More praise for
SNOTTY SAVES THE DAY

"Tod Davies has produced an imaginative book that will make readers think twice: do they know the meaning of fairy tales and of their own lives?"

—**Jack Zipes**, author of *Why Fairy Tales Stick*

"The Arcadians know that real wisdom is found in fairy tales. Look inside this world and find wonder. Thank goodness for Tod Davies, who knows we need fairy tales."

—**Kate Bernheimer,** editor of
My Mother She Killed Me, My Father He Ate Me
and *Fairy Tale Review*

At EXTERMINATING ANGEL PRESS,
we're taking a new approach to our world.
A new way of looking at things.
New stories, new ways to live our lives.
We're dreaming how we want our lives and our world to be…

Also from
EXTERMINATING ANGEL PRESS

THE SUPERGIRLS: *Fashion, Feminism, Fantasy,
and the History of Comic Book Heroines*
by Mike Madrid

JAM TODAY: *A Diary of Cooking
With What You've Got*
by Tod Davies

CORRECTING JESUS: *2000 Years of
Changing the Story*
by Brian Griffith

3 DEAD PRINCES: *An Anarchist Fairy Tale*
by Danbert Nobacon
with illustrations
by Alex Cox

DIRK QUIGBY'S GUIDE TO THE AFTERLIFE
by E. E. King

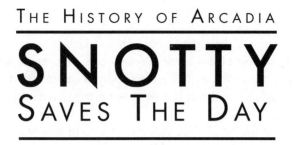

THE HISTORY OF ARCADIA

SNOTTY
SAVES THE DAY

Being a reproduction of
the original Arcadian edition

by
TOD DAVIES

Illustrated by
GARY ZABOLY

EXTERMINATING ANGEL
PRESS

Portions of this book first appeared, some in different form, on the
Exterminating Angel Press online magazine at
www.exterminatingangel.com

EXTERMINATING ANGEL PRESS
"Creative Solutions for Practical Idealists"
Visit *www.exterminatingangel.com* to join the conversation
info@exterminatingangel.com

Exterminating Angel book design by Mike Madrid

ISBN 978-1-935259-07-7
Library of Congress Control Number: 2011922592

Distributed by CONSORTIUM BOOK SALES & DISTRIBUTION
www.cbsd.com

PRINTED IN THE UNITED STATES OF AMERICA

EDITOR'S NOTE

This book came to Exterminating Angel Press in an unusual way. We still don't know entirely what to make of it, though everyone around here feels it should be published, and in its original form.

It was like this: sometime last year, in the late fall, I went out as usual to walk the dogs in the woods behind the house. There's a big tree back there, next to the creek, one that's bigger than all the others, saved from the general logging of the area back at the turn of the twentieth century. It's a fir, and it's so big around that you can't hug it; two people can't even touch fingers if they try to circle it with their arms. It's a favorite tree of mine. I usually stop to greet it in some way as I pass.

This particular morning was an early warning of winter, that first early snowfall that surprises you after a warm day. Everything was white and quiet. As I passed the tree, I looked at it the way I always did. And there, leaning neatly up against the trunk of the giant fir tree, sitting up straight on the snow, was a brown paper and string wrapped parcel.

You can imagine how this isn't a normal sight in the woods behind my house. It's National Forest back there, and hardly anyone walks there but me. So I was curious. And when I bent down to get the package, I saw that it was addressed like this:

To the Publisher of Exterminating Angel Press
located in the woods of the State of Jefferson
in the country of Cascadia

I took it home and opened it.

It was a book. Not just a manuscript, a book. There were stamps on the parcel of a type that I certainly have never seen before. No one I've shown them to can identify them either. There were a lot of them, stuck on haphazardly, the way you do when you're not sure how much postage a package is going to take. Most of them were gold lined around the edges, pictures of mountains and rivers—that kind of thing. Two of them were pictures of a young woman holding a crown. I didn't recognize her.

And there was a note with the book. It claimed the parcel had come to me from another world. Another country in another world.

I asked Alan, our FedEx guy; Jesse, our UPS driver; and Ben, our mailman, if they had any idea where the parcel came from, but all three seemed honestly surprised by the question (except Jesse, who, like all UPS drivers, is too cool to be surprised by anything). So that seems to rule out any kind of regular delivery.

It was later that I remembered that on the night before I found the parcel, I'd heard an owl hooting behind the house. I love owls, so I notice when they hoot. We hadn't heard one for a long time, is why I remember. But I didn't connect it with the parcel. Now, though, I'm not so sure.

In the parcel was a book, a fairy tale, with notes from a scholar, explaining its importance to this other world. I don't know why they sent the book to EAP. The only thing I can think of is that they—and the fairy tale itself—seem to think the Small and Everyday are more important than the Transcendent and the Great. And of course we're completely on side with that.

We decided to publish the book in the form it was sent to us—though we did add our own illustrations, since the ones that came with the original text appear to be pictures from the actual history of Arcadia, and so probably have little meaning to our own audience.

Whether or not Dr. Alan Fallaize was right in entrusting this work to EAP, only time, I guess, will tell.

The Editor

[*What follows is the letter enclosed in the parcel of the book*
The History of Arcadia: Snotty Saves The Day
(also known as the Legendus Snottianicus).]

The Publisher of Exterminating Angel Press
In the land of Cascadia
The state of Oregon
The valley of Colestin

A warm greeting sent to you from Arcadia, and
please forgive the hurried note. I have little
time to send this parcel safely off to you; the
war here means our libraries are in immediate
danger, and we have little time to save certain
key works.

We have tried several times before this to send
other books for response, and to other labora-
tories, universities, governments, worlds. In
fact, we tried several times to send the best
known of our Arcadian works, my own ON THE
DISCOVERY OF BIOLOGICAL TRUTHS IN FAIRY TALES.
Almost every time was a failure. Almost every
time the parcel came back "return to sender."
Except for our fairy tales. Technical works do
not travel well. Stories do.

As for the importance of this story: we believe the late Professor Devindra Vale discovered, right before her death, that SNOTTY SAVES THE DAY is the actual story of real events. We believe she had discovered that what Snotty became literally formed our world.

I've no time to explain further. If the present battle should end in our favor, you'll hear from me again. If not, at least SNOTTY SAVES THE DAY will have found its way to safety. And who knows what happens to Ideas once they find a place in any world.

Yours,

Alan Fallaize

    Dr. Alan Fallaize
    The Tower By The Pond
    St. Vitus's College
    Wrykyn
    ARCADIA

FOR WISDOM

As he walked, though, he started to feel lonely.

THE HISTORY *of* ARCADIA

SNOTTY

SAVES THE DAY

ALSO KNOWN AS
The Legendus Snottianicus

EDITED
by
DR. ALAN FALLAIZE

WITH FOREWORD AND ORIGINAL NOTES
by
PROFESSOR DEVINDRA VALE

ILLUSTRATED

OTTERBRIDGE UNIVERSITY PRESS

First Edition

Published by
OTTERBRIDGE UNIVERSITY PRESS,
at Wrykyn, in Arcadia,
in the year of Sophia the Wise, 83

FOR WISDOM

CONTENTS

A Note from Dr. Alan Fallaize

As Arcadia knows, the late Professor Devindra Vale, at the end of her life, was at work on the final proofs of an annotated edition of SNOTTY SAVES THE DAY. This book, on the surface a mere fairy tale of the adventures of a very unappealing boy, was originally found, though missing key chapters, in the archives at Eisler Hall, as the ancient *Legendus Snottianicus*. Professor Vale, along with Professor Joyanna Bender Boyce-Flood and the students of Bel Regina College, spent years translating the text, only to find the book in its entirety, translated, in the papers of our late queen, Sophia the Wise.

At the time of her death two years ago, Professor Vale was giving the book a further, final study, adding her own scholarly footnotes. Though they are incomplete, we believe they are important enough to warrant inclusion. We have also included an early draft of a foreword that was found among her papers.

May this book move her—our—work forward. May it lead to more answers in this crucial line of inquiry.

I would like to thank Shiva and Walter Todhunter for their support and assistance in preparing this edition. Also thanks to Professors Joyanna Bender Boyce-Flood, Chloe Watson, and Malcolm Sivia for their invaluable comments on the presentation of the manuscript, as well as their aid in compiling a bibliography.

Most especially, my thanks go to the late Professor Devindra Vale, who taught me—at times, in spite of myself—to stay on the side of Truth.

May the side of Truth, always, win in the end.

Alan Fallaize
In the year of Sophia the Wise, 83 AE
St. Vitus's College

Foreword To Snotty Saves The Day
by Professor Devindra Vale

Years ago, before the civil war that presently devastates our country—before, even, the fatal events that led to it—it was my honor to be tasked by our first queen, Lily the Silent, to undertake the immense task of restructuring our educational system. A task indeed! But one which all in Arcadia were aware had been long overdue.

It took more than thirty years. Those of us on the committee were young and idealistic, but by the end of the process we were old. Both Lily the Silent and her daughter the Great Queen, Sophia the Wise, were dead, and our country stood at the brink of disaster. This disaster, we now know with the benefit of hindsight, could have been prevented. But we were blind.

It is the vocation and the duty of the educator to educate. To what purpose? This would seem obvious: to provide a better life for the community. Yet this did not seem obvious to us when we began this task. It does not seem obvious to some of us now.

As is well known, there was one point on which, after laborious research and exhaustive discussion, we all agreed. All of us, scientists, historians, classicists, rhetoricians, mathematicians, and theologians involved in the New Subjectivity, for too long and quite artificially had divided up the world into the parts that formed our disciplines. A series of discoveries in both the sciences and the arts (see Prof. Chloe Watson, *An Elegant Theory of the Contiguity of Theater Arts and Neurobiology* [year 14]; Prof. Joyanna Bender Boyce-Flood, *History or Physics: A False Dichotomy* [year 17 after the Heavy Rains] and *Journey* to the Center of an Illusion [year 25]; Dr. Malcolm Sivia, Connection: A Personal Journey of Discovery, Love, and Loss [year 59], and many more) proved beyond a doubt the essential unity of our world. And this discovery comes in spite of—or perhaps because of—the determined opposition of the followers of Prof. Aspern Grayling (Twelve Points Against the Existence of Unity [year 41]). Alas that the search for truth should have been subordinate to political considerations, but perhaps this is always so, in every world. Perhaps this, too, is a biological truth. It deserves more study, and all of us, all New Subjectivists, should be grateful to the Neofundamentalist school for providing us a whetstone on which to sharpen our thought. And we have thought. We have thought, and we have discovered.

We have discovered through hard data that by studying the world by its parts we had missed the larger truth of its whole. But this discovery may have come too late. There are many who believe that we work in an Ivory Tower that has nothing to do with politics or international affairs. But the new discoveries disprove this. As is usual, the cautious and precise work of the academic world goes too fast for the so-called Men and Women of Action.

If we are too fast for them, we have always been too slow for the world of art. Another key discovery of the First Reign, the key discovery, was this now well-known fact: stories, especially those told to children, hold the greatest secrets of our universe. This is a point I need not belabor, it having been so often and so definitively proved, most concisely in Dr. Alan Fallaize's classic work, On the Discovery of Biological Truths in Fairy Tales (year 61). (Note: see particularly his work on the biological need for equity.)

I myself have spent the last sixty years of my career studying these stories. Of late, my studies and my theorizing have taken on an urgency they lacked in more peaceful times. Long hours, late nights, spent poring over the most ancient texts to be found in the libraries of such bastions of Arcadian civilization as Mumford, Eopolis,

Amaurote, and, of course, Wrykyn, have led me to believe, beyond the shadow of a doubt, that the only possible solution to our present social breakdown is to be found in the old books. *The Legendus Snottianicus*, found in fragments in the archives of Eisler Hall and translated by Prof. Bender Boyce-Flood, hinted that it held a key. When it was discovered that the copy of SNOTTY SAVES THE DAY found in the library of Sophia the Wise after her death was a whole, translated version of the same legend, I knew it needed study of the most profound kind. I have attempted such a study.

Expecting little response from a population in an uproar of xenophobia, fundamentalism, and obsession with a sterile technology (alas that my Neofundamentalist colleagues are included in this condemnation), I nevertheless have decided to publish my findings. No attention will be paid now. But the book will be done, will be distributed in no matter how limited an academic manner, will be there. It will be there for the next generation, no matter how battered, maimed, and small, to read, to use as another tool in the onerous task of digging themselves out of the mire to which we, the present custodians of Arcadia, have led them. The thought of this goes some small way to assuaging the awful guilt that keeps me awake most nights of what should have been a tranquil old age.

If it is not tranquil, it is my own fault.

I should have seen. I should have known. I should have spoken. But, like the rest of us, I was a coward. I was afraid to be wrong. I was afraid to be laughed at. I was afraid to be seen as a fool.

No more.

Here, then, is SNOTTY SAVES THE DAY, long thought to be a minor work by an unknown writer, a story not entirely successful, mainly because of the horrid nature of the hero, the Snotty in question. He is a repellent brat, and what little criticism there has been of this till now mostly ignored work has focused on the difficulty of relating to such a child as the protagonist.

Subsequent scholarship has found, unsettlingly, that it is just the story of this child that is the foundation myth of Arcadia. Just as—in another world we've discovered lies close to our own—Romulus and Remus founded Rome, as King Arthur lies at the bottom of the story of their England, so Snotty is at the bottom of our story. What happens to him is what happened to us.

This is the place to say I suspect more. What I suspect, but cannot yet prove, would rock our foundation. And can I, despite my duties as a scholar, take that responsibility? It is difficult, if not impossible to know. What I will say here is: Snotty is Arcadia. Until we know him, we do not know ourselves. Until we know ourselves, we can never free ourselves from the cycle of vengeance and terror that ravages our once beautiful land.

My heart is heavy with sadness for Arcadia as I read the final proofs of SNOTTY SAVES THE DAY, the book that is, in truth, the first book in the history of Arcadia. The footnotes are meant to be of use to my academic colleagues in further research, but may be ignored by the merely curious reader who wants to see what happens next in the story.

I urge the reader: don't give up on Snotty. His adventures prove that if even one person knows who he or she really is, whole worlds can change. Ours did.

And I urge my colleagues: continue the research. It may be, even, that the study of SNOTTY SAVES THE DAY and of other folk and fairy tales might lead to the answer to the one great remaining question of Arcadian science—why it is that our history begins only eighty-one years ago, and why even those who lived in the time before that have no clear idea of the sequence of events before that time. This has always been the puzzle, of the type that ambitious graduate students dream of solving, and that is ignored, perhaps in frustration, by older and wiser scientists. Who knows but that an answer to this strange conundrum may be found, as so many other truths have been found, in fairy tales and legends such as these. Who knows what answers to other, even more intractable, problems might not be discovered through finding the true solution. I urge my colleagues, all my students, don't cease looking for the truth! I will do what I can, but my time is running out. Already, tonight, in my tower at Wrykyn, overlooking the Lily Pond, I can hear the explosions coming near—too near. And I am very tired.

My thanks, as always, to the Senior Common Room of St Vitus's College, Otterbridge University, and especially to Dr. Alan Fallaize, Professor Malcolm Sivia, and Professor Joyanna Bender Boyce-Flood. And to my beloved great-granddaughter Shiva Todhunter: may the landscapes you paint be peaceful in the future, and may you teach my great-great-granddaughter Devindra the ways of Sophia the Wise.

Professor Devindra Vale
The Tower By The Pond
St. Vitus's College
Otterbridge University
Wrykyn
Arcadia

For Sophia

Prologue

An Angel flew through the dark blue sky between the stars, heading for a planet no other Angel[1] had visited for years. This was a tiny world in a faraway corner of one of the smallest universes in the cosmos. It was a long way away from the center of heaven, so she had plenty of time to contemplate her plan. The other Angels were appalled when she told them what she meant to do. They had long since given up on the place themselves and left it to the Enemy. Why not? It was so ugly. Angels dislike ugliness. They see no point in it.

Once the planet had been a beautiful one, blue and green and white and gold. But now it was mean and shabby: brown and gray and pinched looking, half-hidden under a yellow haze. As the Angel drew closer, she could see the grid of concrete and tarmac streets that covered it, not only on land, but on what had once been seas, canyons, mountains—even icebergs. She winced at this, at the waste and fecklessness and sheer stupidity the landscape showed. She

---

1 Proven conclusively to exist (see Prof. Joyanna Bender Boyce-Flood, *Journey to the Center of an Illusion*, Otterbridge University Press, year 25, chapters 7 and 12). Work still needs to be done on their origins or function. Professor Aspern Grayling's speculation that Angels are a parallel but useless life form is of great interest as a leaping off point for more study, and can be said to be at the heart of the differences between his Neofundamentalist school and that of the New Subjectivity. (See Grayling, *Twelve Points Against the Existence of Unity*, Otterbridge University Press, year 41.) As often noted before, the differences between the folk tales of the imperial Megalopolis that surrounds us and our own Arcadian ones are relevant to this question. Angels are almost unknown in Megalopolitan tales, with the exception of the folk tale "Why the Angels Left"; they are common, however, in those of Arcadia. (See Prof. Devindra Vale, *Folk Tales of Megalopolis and Arcadia: A Comparative Study*, Otterbridge University Press, year 22.)

(1)

wondered at the Enemy. He delighted in just this kind of ugliness and confusion, but as an Angel, of course, she couldn't understand why.

She had long since given up trying to understand what possible pleasure the Enemy[2] could take in the misery and degradation of the many peoples under his rule. He took it—that was enough. She wouldn't worry about why. She would just fight.

She would fight, she thought. And she would choose the battleground, not him. She had lost to him once, when she had made the mistake of letting him choose. Angels do not like to lose. Nothing can kill an Angel, of course, but nothing is more painful to one than the triumphant laugh of the Enemy.

This Angel had heard that laugh. She would hear it for Eternity. This was why she was determined, now, to fight—and in a place where he had long been left to reign supreme. Whether or not she would win, she would fight.

Because the Angel had her Idea. And her Idea was this: "Where the Enemy is, there must be Resistance. No matter how small or poor or funny, it must be there."[3] This was the Law of Everywhere. The Angel had learned it at her Tutor's knee. The Law of Everywhere was everywhere the same. It taught that the best warriors against the Enemy always come from the most despised portion of any world.

---

2   Prof. Grayling's point that no Enemy can or could exist is instructive in this context. Dr. Malcolm Sivia posits that physical nature must possess an evil force working within it, but whether this force is personified or merely symbolic has yet to be determined. (See Sivia, *Connection: A Personal Journey of Discovery, Loss, and Love*, Otterbridge University Press, year 59.) The views of the late Queen Sophia that this force is personified and active in Arcadian conflicts are well known.

3   See Prof. Joyanna Bender Boyce-Flood, *History or Physics: A False Dichotomy*, Otterbridge University Press, year 17, for discussion of the Law of the Small. Her discovery that at the end of every great historical cycle a renewal must take place that begins in the most apparently useless part of the system involved shows a remarkable similarity to this stated "Law of Everywhere."

So the Angel knew very well what she had to do, as she sank beneath the top layer of the yellow haze. Tilting parallel to the earth, and opening her wings to their full breadth, she shot through the smoke, the screaming, and the sirens coming up from the surface, and flew to where she knew the tip of the Resistance there would hide. She knew it would be in the ugliest, the meanest, the shabbiest, and the most cast-off of places. And it was to this place she flew now.

Chapter I

SNOTTY

Hamercy Street ran downhill from the highest point in Widdleshift, which was in the neighborhood of Makewater, which was in the district of Hackendosh, which was part of the county of Queerspittle. All of these were in the far northwest of what had once been the nation of Albion, but which was now known, in the great city of Megalopolis, as East New York.[4]

On Hamercy Street there lived a boy named Snotty. It was an ugly name, and he was an ugly boy. He had very big ears and a very big nose, and very little everything else. He was dusty colored and his eyes were red. His teeth were crooked and his elbows and knees stuck out of everything he wore, no matter how new or old—although his clothes were mostly old and didn't fit him anyway.[5]

Inside of him was ugly, too. Inside of him was moldy and dusty and like it was filled with broken furniture and garbage. So he hardly ever looked inside. You wouldn't have either, if you were Snotty.

Outside of him was not much better. Hamercy Street was mean and ugly and cold and wretched, and Snotty lived at the top of it, in a

---

4   Despite much archival research in search of such a neighborhood in the history of Megalopolis, no record has been found to date. The description fits folk tales that place the Arcadian village of Cockaigne, childhood home of Lily the Silent, inside Megalopolis. See "The Three Tailors," an Arcadian folk tale of three small businessmen in Cockaigne who meet and beat a Megalopolitan devil, using nothing but their wits and a small hand puppet.

5   See above, footnote 3, re: the Law of the Small. Snotty is the most insignificant and contemptible figure in all Arcadian mythology. An unlikely hero.

very ugly house, with his mother—who was no oil painting herself. He didn't see much of her. She spent a lot of her time downstairs, on the pea green settee in front of the broken electric fire, watching TV with a can of lager in her hand. This—along with getting up once in awhile, yawning, and scratching her backside—pretty much constituted her career. She and Snotty had started out well enough when he was born and had shared a few laughs, and of course she felt more warmly toward him as he grew older and was able to pay rent. She liked the added income—on time and everything. Even though he was only twelve years old, Snotty was very punctual about business matters.

"I've got the best kid on all of Hamercy Street," his mother bragged, sitting for a change on the tilting stoop of her house, of course still clutching her can of lager. "The best AND the smartest. Pays me rent and everything. Not like your useless bunch."

The other mothers grunted at this. One of them, her dearest pal, gave Snotty's mother a vicious look before taking herself inside and slamming the door after. The door was broken, and fell off its top hinge, which spoiled the effect. This made Snotty's mother laugh so hard that the beer came out of her nose.[6]

"What's with her?" she said as she wiped the beer off her face with the back of her hand.

"Don't know," shrugged one of the other mothers. "She's been on a rag ever since that kid of hers got shot by the cops."

"What, still? " Snotty's mother said cheerfully. "That was—must've been at least a month ago. AND he was a stupid kid. God."

"She liked him though," someone else said in a reflective way.

"Well, I mean, get over it," Snotty's mother said.

"Yeah."

They sat there in the gathering gloom, and after awhile there

---

6   The motif of beer coming from the nose is a common one in folk tales, both Arcadian and Megalopolitan. See particularly "How Beer Was Invented," and that favorite of naughty Arcadian children "Who Will Find a Pot to Piss In?" (See Vale, year 22.)

didn't seem to be much to say. So Snotty's mother took herself off, too, braying up the stairs as she went back to her pea green settee: "Snotty? You up there or what?"

There was no answer. It didn't matter. Snotty's mother didn't care. She went to the pea green settee, and, flopping herself on it, began to pick at a scab on her heel. She chortled as she remembered her neighbor's face. "Got her good," she thought. It was enough to keep Snotty's mother happy for weeks, upsetting her friend that way. She yawned, satisfied with herself and her world, and with the half empty can of lager in her hand, curled up on the settee and snored. After a moment, the can tipped over and fell. As Snotty's mother grunted, a line of stale beer snaked out over the worn carpet, following the warp of the floor to the bottom of the stair, which itself snaked up, listing and leaning, with a rattly old railing you wouldn't want to lean on, all the way to a shifty little landing made out of cracked pieces of wood.

It was on this landing that Snotty stood, his tiny hand on the splintery wood of the railing. He listened hard until he heard his mother snore. And then he turned and went inside the attic door. His footstep was light—so light that it barely left a print, even in the fine dirt of the back alley off Hamercy Street—and he didn't make a sound.

"This is the last time I'll stand here," Snotty thought to himself, looking around the attic—his room—with a dispassionate eye. "The very last time."

Snotty had determined to leave his ugly little house and his ugly little room, and, really, looking at it, you wouldn't have wanted to stay either. It was a desolate space. It was moldy and cold, and the wind whistled in through the cracked windowpane. One naked bulb lit the whole, worked by a greasy switch. In the corner, in front of a bricked up fireplace, lay a single mattress topped by a crumpled sleeping bag.

There were no toys, unless you counted one dirty bit of yellow and black battered plush that lay shoved over between the dirty mattress and the floor. It might have been the remains of a teddy bear. Then again, it might not. It was hard to tell.[7]

"Can't say I'm going to miss it much," Snotty said, shrugging to himself. And I don't think anyone would have missed it much, either. Except that Snotty was only twelve years old, and this was the only room he had ever known.

He went over to the window for one last look out over Widdleshift. It was dark and it was gray and it was scattered with rusting iron fences and yellowing patches of grass on which pieces of broken glass sparkled in the twilight. The dirty brick houses huddled together, tilting this way and that. This was the only sight that Snotty had ever known.

"Or that, either," Snotty said, trying to keep his courage up. He was mean and ugly, but he was brave, too. You have to be brave to leave your home when it's time to go, even if that home is mean and ugly.

Snotty lingered, then, for a minute, but not because he was afraid. He stayed to look at a sight that had long puzzled him, off and on, when he had the time to be puzzled—which was not often, given the business interests that would tonight, he hoped, be taking him to a more ambitious field of action altogether.

---

7   The Teddy Bear is an important motif in Arcadian fairy tales. See my *A Short History of the Fairy Tale (with excerpts from the Legendus Snottianicus)*, Otterbridge University Press, year 26. Teddy Bears have long held a strange fascination for Arcadians, a fact noted, not without contempt, by Professor Aspern Grayling. (See Grayling, year 41.) Grayling refers specifically to "the essential inferiority of the provincial Arcadian mind to the imperial Megalopolitan: its childish love of play, its obsession with festival, its affection for toys and pets of all kinds." Grayling contrasts this to the Megalopolitan "aestheticism, use of food and drink for ceremonial rather than festive purposes, as well as its manly love of sport."

"Six houses," he said to himself. "But seven gardens. Why should it be like that? When everybody knows that six houses should have six gardens."

Because that was what he could see, from his attic room, at the top of Hamercy Street. In the middle of the street, in the part where it leveled off before heading on to the church and the pub and the police station, there were six mean little dirty brown brick houses. But behind them, in a back alley—an alley, incidentally, that Snotty knew very well—there were seven gardens. He could see from where he stood that the gardens were mingy and wretched, covered with broken glass and rotting, creosote-soaked lumber, matted with a tangle of nettles, dandelions, and stunted blackberry leaves. But that wasn't the problem. The problem was that there were too many of them.

"Six houses. Seven gardens." Snotty shook his head. "It's not right."

But after tonight, he would never see those houses or those gardens again. He brightened at the thought. So there was really no use worrying about them. And since Snotty very rarely did anything that was of no use to him—he couldn't remember the last time, in fact—now he put the gardens and the houses out of his mind. And lifted up a heavy, frayed backpack onto his scrawny little back.

His cool eyes raked the miserable room one last time. Then he turned off the one light, and went out, closing the door behind him.[8]

---

8 Note the traditional motif of Rejected One Who Sets Out Into the World (see Vale, year 26). This appears most notably in the Cockaigne Idiot Cycle: "The Idiot Goes Up the Mountains," "The Idiot Goes Down to the Marsh," and the most popular of the stories, "The Idiot Flies to the Moon." All these classic Arcadian tales tell the story of a girl supposed to be an Idiot, though the action of each story shows, of course, that she is anything but. These were the favorite tales of our second queen, Sophia the Wise. I have had the personal experience of hearing her spirited renditions of these tales to a group of Arcadian children (including my own great-granddaughter), which our queen would always conclude by saying, "And who was the REAL idiot?" to the children's great delight.

"Evening, Snot," a small boy said as he swept a bit of glass out of our hero's way. "Nice night, isn't it?" His face shone in the darkness with an expression of anxious deference. Snotty was something of a legend to the smaller ones on Hamercy Street, and the boy timidly hoped for a word of encouragement from his hero.

Snotty ignored him. One of the first lessons he had learned on Hamercy Street was that kindness equals weakness. He never made the mistake of being nice to anyone smaller or more helpless than himself. So he passed the small boy by as if he hadn't even seen him, and speeded up his already fast pace. So energetic, purposeful, and efficient was his stride that if he hadn't been scrawny, ragged, and just twelve, he might have been mistaken for a district manager on his way to a very important meeting. The smaller boy looked after him with helpless admiration, vowing to be like him some day.

Snotty's energy and purpose and efficiency faltered only once, and that was down in front of the six houses that fronted the alley of Back Hamercy Street. Here, unable to help himself, he stopped and stared and frowned.

He looked at the houses and counted them. There were definitely six. Six houses. Even though he had better things to think about, this positively annoyed him. Then he noticed a paint-peeled Garden Gnome leering at him from the weeds in front of the sixth house. Snotty aimed a kick at the Gnome's head and stomped it efficiently into the cracked concrete of the pavement.

He felt better after that and continued on his way.

———

"BZZZZZTTT."

Snotty walked onto the waste ground that lined the other side of Hamercy Street and ducked under the phone mast there. It spat out a thin blue light as he passed.

"BZZZZZTTT."

On the other side of the phone mast was a billboard. On this billboard, fading and peeling as it was, was pictured the beautiful face of the most beautiful young man in the world. He was elegant and slim and dressed in creamy white. His skin was tan and his hair was luxuriant and black. His teeth were pearly. His nose was straight. His eyes were the color of turquoise. His hands were in his pockets, and he was laughing. And over his head was just one word: BIG.[9]

He was cool and elegant and young and strong, even with a strip of paper peeled off his side. Snotty paused for a moment to gaze up at him.

"I'm going where you are," Snotty said to himself. And the young man locked eyes with him and seemed to understand. As if some message had been sent and received, Snotty picked up his pace and, with a renewed sense of purpose, strode into the darkness ahead.

"BZZZZZTTT."

Behind him, the thin blue light from the phone mast flashed again.

It lit up the waste ground with a faint and sickly glow, and Snotty could see five boys his own age standing around the cracked, weed-infested concrete of a schoolyard. They stared dejectedly at an object on the ground.

An old man lay there, moaning and clutching at his head, his pockets turned inside out. The boys had robbed him. But he had

---

9   Prof. Grayling has noted, in earlier private conversation, that this is often the 'description of the imaginary Enemy.' I am indebted to him for the insight, though our disagreement about the scientific meaning of the word 'imaginary' continues, even as we face each other from opposite sides of the present civil war.

been a disappointment.

Snotty stopped to have a look. One of the boys held out the handful of change they'd gotten for their trouble. The others looked away, ashamed. They knew what a successful businessman like Snotty would think of this kind of profit margin.

"That's it?" Snotty said, disgusted. He shook his head. "You guys should go in for another line of work. You're no good at this one."

There was an embarrassed pause. "Well," said one of the boys finally, wiping his nose on his sleeve, "it'll be better when we're old enough to join the Police."[10]

"It's your own stupid fault," Snotty scolded, and the boys hung their heads. "Who do you think is going to come by this place, the amount of times you've robbed somebody here? Show a little innovation! Try somewhere else for a change!"

The shamed expressions on the boys' faces turned to smiles as this advice went home.

"Thanks, Snot," one of the boys said gruffly, holding out his hand. Snotty gravely shook it, and then shook hands all around. And the boys went into a huddle to construct a new business plan.

Snotty smiled a superior little smile and continued on his way.

One of the boys—his name was Stan—ran after him. (At this, the old man on the ground took advantage of the opportunity to crawl off the playground into the shelter of the boy's toilet, where he would wait until two mornings later, when the school's half-pay janitor would find him and call the fire brigade.)

Stan caught up with Snotty and grabbed at his arm. "Put in a

---

10   This is, in fact, an accurate depiction of the work force that historically has formed the Megalopolitan police, now known as the National Peace Force. It is instructive to note its place in this Arcadian Fairy Tale, since the actual Megalopolitan Peace Force has a history of occupying Arcadia when it can. The Peace Force is presently advising the Neofundamentalist side of our civil war. Professor Grayling has made no secret of his admiration for its structure, function, and effectiveness.

good word for me with your boss," Stan pleaded. "Put in a good word for me with Mr. Big."

Snotty wheeled around, hands on his hips. "You've got no head for business," he said shortly. "That's a fact. Why would I tell Mr. Big about you?"

Now, it was one of Snotty's achievements that he was known to be the personal runner of Mr. Big himself. No one knew how the rumor got started—Snotty was always tight-lipped about his own business—but nobody doubted it was true.

"I've got a good arm on me," Stan whined. "And I'm loyal, really I am. You know you've always been my role model."

Snotty turned again and gave Stan a look.

"All right," he said. "I'll see what I can do." Snotty thought that Stan might come in useful someday. You never knew.

"Aw, thanks, Snot, you're a real pal," Stan said. But his eyes were hard, and he might have decided to give his role model a thump just for old time's sake, if it wasn't for a shout now that went up from the other boys on the playground.

A dog had appeared, all gray and black with a huge maw, and the boys chased it around the schoolyard. Stan's eyes gleamed at this. He would have been off to join them if Snotty hadn't grabbed him by the sleeve.

"Let go, Snot," Stan said. "Look, it's a dog."

"Listen," Snotty said, hanging onto Stan's jacket. "I just remembered. Doesn't your aunt live in the middle of Hamercy Street?"

Stan nodded, annoyed at being kept back. The rest of the boys chased the howling dog. "Yeah, sure. The house with the Garden Gnome. She loves that Garden Gnome."

"Listen," Snotty insisted again. Stan was straining to be off, but Snotty held him there. "Listen," he repeated. "Six houses there, right?" Stan nodded again. "Then how come there's seven gardens behind?"

But Stan wasn't listening. He yanked his arm away from Snotty and ran off to where the boys had the dog cornered. It cowered against what was left of a rusting chain link fence.

Snotty, expressionless, let him go. He continued, with his usual sense of purpose, along his way. The howls of the dog followed him, but he never allowed anything like that to distract him from business, and it was to a business meeting that he headed now.

Chapter II

AT THE CROWN AND MITRE

"Wh-wh-why c-c-can't he b-b-be like other b-b-b-boys?" Mick complained the way he always did after he finished his third pint of watery beer. He was sitting, as he always did on a Wednesday, with Keef and Dodger in the back room of the Crown and Mitre pub on Hamercy Street. They were waiting, as they always were, for Snotty.

"He needs a good thumping," said Keef, his tiny pig eyes shining malevolently, the way they always did behind his thick wire-rimmed glasses. "One of us should give it to him." At this he looked at Mick.

"Then he WOULD be like all the other boys," chortled Dodger, the way he always did. In his amusement, he, too, snorted his lager the wrong way and spewed a little bit out his nose. (This happened a lot on Hamercy Street. In fact, it was practically a sport.)[11] "That's what boys are for. I know I got thumped all the time, and look how I turned out."

Mick and Keef turned and looked at Dodger. It didn't seem to either of them that having been thumped when he was young had done Dodger much good. But they kept this thought to themselves.

"That's beside the point," Keef said impatiently.

"Wh-wh-what is the p-p-p-p..."

Dodger laughed again. More beer spurted out of his nose.

"P-p-p-p-POINT?"

"The point," Keef said patiently, "is that he has money. And that money by rights belongs to us."

"How do you figure?" said Dodger curiously.

---

11 See note 6 above.

"It's obvious. We're bigger than he is. And we're stronger."

"Th-th-that's tr-tr-true."

Keef leaned confidentially across the grubby table. "So here," he said, "is what we are going to do."

———————

The Crown and Mitre pub was a villainous and lonely place at the end of Hamercy Street. It had once been held up on both sides by other, even older buildings—a Mission Hall and a Library—but these had long since been torn down. Now it tilted by itself over a scruffy dirt square that was covered with broken glass.[12]

Snotty turned into its splintered doorway and contemplated a sign hanging there. This said: NO DOGS. NO CHILDREN. NO EXCEPTIONS.

Snotty stared at this for a moment. Then he went inside. He shifted his backpack onto one shoulder, and a couple of packages wrapped in Christmas paper poked out.

"He's a cool one," a policeman snorted from the parked car across the street. His name was Terry, and his partner's name was Alan.[13] "And what's with those packages?" Terry had the wild look of a man who has been sent to the wrong place by mistake, and who keeps trying to get someone in authority to fix it. Alan was more resigned: he was older and burlier and sadder, too.

Alan sighed. He watched two toddlers play a game on the sidewalk

———————

12 I myself can assert, from personal childhood experience, that this is an accurate depiction of a typical lower class neighborhood in Megalopolis. But no record exists of Hamercy Street, which must be assumed to be fictional.

13 Alan is an uncommon given name in Megalopolis—I've been unable to find records of more than three there over the last eighty years. But it is a common one in Arcadia, where it was the name of the famous freedom fighter and father-by-adoption of our first queen, Lily the Silent.

with a broken beer bottle. He was feeling more depressed by the minute.

"I'll tell you what's in the packages," he said, tilting his head backward so he could stare at the ceiling of the car, which was, he thought, a nice change from the world outside. "What he has to sell. And what, you ask"—though Terry hadn't—"does a little boy in a place like this have to sell? It's drugs, of course. No need to say what. A little of this, a little of that. He gets it down at the docks and then hides the stuff in dolls, Easter eggs, Christmas presents—depends on the time of year. When we catch him, which we do from time to time, he says some strange man gave the packages to him. What's the court going to say? He's not more than twelve years old, and he looks about eight." Alan gave a grudging laugh. "None of us thought it was true for years. Didn't think it was possible for the kid to have the kind of brains to think something like that up."[14]

Terry snorted again and grabbed the car's wheel as if he'd forgotten it wasn't going anywhere. "I don't think much of the kind of brains that lead to criminal behavior," he spat.

Alan sank further into his seat, still staring at the ceiling. He knew Terry's type well. Always in a hurry. Always trying to start things or stop things. Always thinking he COULD start or stop things.

Alan himself had long ago given up trying to start things or stop things. In fact, he had few illusions about his impact on anything around him at all.

He sighed again. He didn't want to have an impact. What he really wanted was a drink.

---

14   The motif of a small child selling drugs to earn money and prestige is a common one in Megalopolitan folk tales. (See Vale, year 22.) In Megalopolitan folk tales, the hero—for it is always a hero, never a heroine, who figures in this motif—goes on from a start as a drug peddler to become a celebrity of some kind: a politician, a successful businessman, or a media magnate. Such a motif is unknown in Arcadian folk/fairy tales, with the single exception of *Snotty Saves the Day*.

The owner of the Crown and Mitre had, like Alan, long ago given up thinking he could have any kind of influence on anything around him, and so felt helpless whenever he looked at his horrible pub. The lounge's moldy orange-brown carpet, the stained and torn fake leather banquettes, the cheap veneer peeling off the walls, the tilting pool table with its broken leg propped up by a stack of beer mats: this was the Crown and Mitre. It had always been like this. It would always be like this. What could he do about it?

Instead of worrying, he watched the television that blared from one corner of the room. It was a way to pass the time. He was used to it. So when Snotty walked in, he was annoyed at being interrupted. Without turning, he barked, "Hey! No kids!" Then, seeing who it was, "Oh. It's you." He held out a hand, which Snotty shook in a businesslike way. "They're waiting for you," he said, jerking his thumb toward the back room. "Just like always." Then he went back to his television show, a Lifestyle Presentation touring the Central New York home of the Duke of New York.[15]

Snotty stood for a moment, eyes narrowed, taking in the Duke's way of life: the indoor swimming pool, the marble foyer, the silk-covered walls, the bath's gold spigots in the shape of swans. Together these details made up a vision so desirable, so delightful, so different from anything that Snotty knew that he drifted into a momentary dream.

He shook himself awake, of course, back to the business at hand. But it was to prove a fatal distraction. Snotty had come into this pub so many times the same way, exchanging the same handshake with the

---

15   Central New York, as we all know, does, in fact, exist as a neighborhood in Megalopolis. Or rather, it did in the days before the Great Flood and Great Migration, when so many of us living in Megalopolis emigrated over the mountains to Arcadia. Central New York was, in fact, the home of the father of Queen Sophia the Wise.

owner, going into the same back room, doing business with the same men, that he wasn't paying the attention that he should.

There they were, Mick, Keef, and Dodger, drinking lager just like they always did.

"H-h-hello, Sn-snotty," Mick said, his dirty toenails sticking out of his sandals just like they always did.

"Evening, Snot," Keef said, his little squinty eyes gleaming as usual in his fat pink face.

"Your favorite drink, Snotty, just the way you like it," Dodger said in his ingratiating voice, the way he always did. And there, as always, was the waiting can of sweet soda pop and a cloudy glass of ice.

And Snotty, the way he always did, pulled the Christmas packages out of his backpack and exchanged them for bundles of cash. But his head was filled, not with the cold realities of commerce, but with pleasant thoughts of roast chicken, strawberry ice cream, feather pillows, and the Duke of New York asking his business advice.

From which it is clear that Snotty was finding it harder and harder to keep his mind on his job. To tell the truth, he had taken it as far as it could go. It didn't offer him any more scope. He was bored with the whole thing.

As usual, Mick tried to stiff him. By now it was a familiar game they all played, and everyone had a good laugh when Snotty counted Mick's bundle and found the usual one bill missing. Mick, as usual, pretended he'd miscounted, then tried to borrow the money first from Snotty, then from Keef and Dodger. He finally, grudgingly, scraped together just enough from the change in his pockets. Just like he always did.

None of their hearts were in any of this. With a sigh, Snotty collected his cash and turned to go.

He didn't notice that Keef took Mick aside and muttered something. Or that Dodger ushered him to the door with an even more than usually obsequious gloat. If he had, it would have made him think. But his thoughts were drifting. He had grown tired of Hamercy Street. He was going stale. He needed new challenges, a change of scene.

Yes, it was time for a change, all right. It was definitely time for a change.

Terry saw Snotty come out of the pub, and hit Alan on the arm.

"Calm down," Alan advised him wearily. Against all regulations, he lit a cigarette. "He'll go to stash his money now. We'll pick him up there." Terry grunted agreement to this and sank back into his seat. "You know the boy's game?" Alan said, pointing his cigarette at Snotty as he disappeared down the street. "He pretends he's the go-between. Pretends he works for Mr. Big. There is no Mr. Big. That child is it. You know what he does, Terry..." At this, Alan leaned forward, eyes bright, as if he could see it all. "That boy...that CHILD goes down to the docks on his own. Tells the men there that his father sent him. Or his uncle. Or his brother. He buys the stuff cheap, brings it up here, distributes it himself. And he's twelve years old! Think of it!"[16]

But Terry didn't think. He growled instead.

Alan was too caught up in his own vision to care. "Think of the BRAIN," he said, his eyes gleaming in the dark. "Think of the

---

16   Again, the Small Child as Criminal Mastermind is a common motif in Megalopolitan folk tales. See "Rudyard the Magician," where the hero begins as a con artist and goes on to world-wide fame as a conjuror. Or "Anthony Saves the World," in which the plagiarist hero ends by patriotically killing the enemies of Megalopolis with his dark skills. Or "The Jesting Pilates," where the hero, drug dealer turned physician, saves an entire continent from a dread disease. Megalopolis, of course, has no known fairy tales: by which I mean tales that include any world other than Megalopolis. Its oral tradition is entirely confined, imaginatively speaking, within its own borders, and the borders of those lands that it has invaded.

willpower! The nerve! Think of it, Terry. Could you have done anything like that when you were a kid? Could I?"

Terry gave Alan a disgusted look. Alan was going soft. Terry planned on reporting this at the right time to the right authorities, after which, with Alan gone, he, Terry, would move up in the hierarchy. In the meantime he had to keep his focus. He wished Alan would shut up so that he could concentrate on the job.

But Alan wasn't done yet. "I look around this place," he said. "I look at it and I think: the kids who're stealing, setting fire to buildings, breaking car windows—they're angry."

The combination of Alan's philosophizing and Terry's distracted annoyance meant that neither of them noticed Mick come out of the Crown and Mitre and follow Snotty down the street.

"Those kids," Alan said, still deep in his own thoughts, "they've got reason to be angry. At least they're not beaten down, sitting at home watching television and letting their brains turn to mush. Maybe the angry ones can change this stinking world."[17] Here he winced at the unlikeliness of such an event. "Somehow," he trailed off.

Terry started up the car. "I like the world the way it is, thanks," he said. "Tell me where we're going, would you, please?"

Alan sighed again and pointed ahead. "Up there," he said. "Back Hamercy Street." And the car lurched away.

---

17   Here is another of those differences of which I spoke. No Megalopolitan tale of any kind indicates sympathy with the idea of 'changing the world.' Whether there is a difference between Megalopolitan biology and Arcadian, or this is simply an example of determined censorship through the ages, I leave for future scholarship to determine.

Chapter III

IN THE SEVENTH GARDEN

And all that time, the Seventh Garden waited behind the six houses on Hamercy Street.

The alley of Back Hamercy Street was an L-shaped dirt path that curved around the houses in front of it, and it was here that Snotty went now. "This is the last time," he thought as he walked into its shadows and heard the familiar sound of water dripping—plop, plop—down the fences and the walls. A rusted skip sank into the dirt at the side of the lane. It waited there for him, buried to its belly in dirt and filth, stewing in old rags, yellowed newspapers, and bits of barbed wire.

Snotty's look softened. This was familiar. It was what he knew. "Now then," he scolded himself. "Don't start going sentimental on me." There would be other skips, he knew, in other towns—bigger and better skips, and filled with a higher quality trash, too.

With that in mind, Snotty now set to work, methodically digging in a special, particularly disgusting spot marked by an old green and gold coffee can. It didn't take long for him to uncover a battered metal box, flaking red and gray paint, which he opened. He gave a contented sigh.

The box was full of money.[18] Snotty scooped this up and would have stuffed it in his pockets—except there was this sound.

Instinctively he shoved the money back in the box, and shoved the box back under the trash. Then he looked around.

---

18 A common motif in folk, fairy, and all other kinds of tales in all languages, in all worlds. No reference needed

That was when he saw the dog. It was standing there, quiet. It stared at him.

"Hey there," Snotty said in an uneasy voice. "Heh, heh." But the dog just stood there staring.

"What are you looking at?" Snotty was annoyed at being interrupted, but he was curious, too. The dog was covered with blood-matted fur, the result of its recent encounter with Stan and the boys.

"Go on," Snotty muttered halfheartedly. "Shoo." He and the dog looked at each other. Snotty couldn't help being impressed by how big it was, and how it just stood there looking at him. The whole thing excited him in a way he couldn't figure out, so he did what he usually did when in doubt. He picked up a rock and threw it.

The rock hit the dog's side with a dull thud, and Snotty tensed, getting ready to run, and eyeing the exact fence over which he reckoned he could get a good head start. But the dog, to his surprise, didn't chase him. It didn't even growl. It just put its head down and gave a deep sigh. Then it shook its large and shaggy gray-black head and sighed again.

"What's your problem?" Snotty said defensively. He already knew that throwing the rock was a mistake, but experience had taught him never to apologize.[19] Instead he looked down at the ground resentfully and scratched his head.

The dog just looked at him. Snotty looked back. And the dog, still looking at him over its massive shoulder, trotted down the alley of Back Hamercy Street and stopped at the door of the Seventh Garden. It cocked its head.

"No," Snotty said firmly. "I'm not coming down there. There's something spooky about that garden." In spite of himself, he counted the gardens again. One... two... three... four... five... six... seven...

Seven gardens.

---

19   Another common motif in Megalopolitan folk tales, though rare in those of Arcadia. See note 16.

Six houses.

Seven gardens.

The dog barked. Snotty backed up a step.

The dog barked again.

A wind blew, and the door to the Seventh Garden opened. The wind rushed through the alley, right into Snotty's face.

Snotty had backed up another step, planning to turn and run, when the wind blew over him, and with it, its smells. These were layers of smells, all of them good. One was of warm taffy apples, one of buttered corn, one of coffee and cream.

Snotty had never smelled any of these things. Startled, he took a step forward. The smells multiplied. Cinnamon. Tomato sauce. Lemon and sage. You and I have smelled these things, but Snotty— never. Sniffing, Snotty followed them until he was at the open door of the Seventh Garden. He sniffed again. There was no doubt. The smells came from inside.[20]

"How about that, Dog?" Snotty said, peering into the dim shadows of the garden. But the dog was gone. At any rate, it was nowhere to be seen.

"Are you there?" Snotty said. There was no answer. Just a rustling noise that came from all the overgrown corners of the Seventh Garden. A gold light flickered behind this rustle, and the green tangle of weeds and flowers and vines heaved in a slow moving tide. The trees leaned forward toward Snotty, their branches waving. But there was no wind now.

---

20 Good smells are a common Arcadian motif, though rare in Megalopolitan tales. (See Vale, year 26.) See, for example, "The Baker's Stone," where, at the request of his mother, a kindly baker is granted the magic ability to make as much delicious bread as is needed for a wedding party that has run out; "Calendula the Cat," where a cat and a dog are shown by an angel why they were given different senses of smell; and "The Kith of the Fairy Forest," where a starving child obtains wonderful food by singing to wake his fairy protectors from sleep.

"I don't think I like this," Snotty said. Even as he said it, though, he knew it wasn't true. He did like it. He didn't know why. Something here was familiar, as if it were a place he knew very well from sometime long ago.

While he pondered this, another smell floated past. This was a smell it's almost impossible to describe. It was a mixture of violets and morning sunlight after a rain and white velvet and puppies, and the out and out unexpectedness of it filled Snotty with panic. "That's it for me," he thought, stumbling backward. "I'm out of here." In his hurry to get away he almost fell, but he got his balance back and ran down the alley to Hamercy Street, where Mick, unfortunately, was waiting. Snotty ran slap into him.

"G-got you!" Mick said, wrapping his stubby arms around our hero and squeezing for all he was worth. Snotty, smothering there, smelled tar and sweat and stale beer.[21] With a muffled shout, he shoved as hard as he could, and brought one scrawny knee up harder.

Mick yowled and let go. Snotty raced back the way he came.

But Mick, who was faster than he looked, caught up with him right outside the Seventh Garden. With an angry bellow, he pounced and brought Snotty down in the dirt, both of them shouting and coughing. Snotty pummeled Mick on the chest, but as his fists were extremely little, this didn't count for much. So instead he yelled as loud as he could.

Alan and Terry, getting out of their car on Hamercy Street, heard this and ran. Terry shouted. Alan shouted, too.

There was a lot of shouting at this point in the story.

"Other side," Alan shouted. He meant Terry should block their exit out the other end of the alley. And this Terry sprinted to do.

Mick cursed. Snotty tried to push him off. But it was no use. So instead he shouted some more. Mick shouted back.

---

21 Bad smells are a common Megalopolitan motif, but rare in Arcadian tales. The examples are too numerous to mention here.

"Okay," Alan said more quietly now that he was near. "That's enough, now. Give it up."

"A f-f-fine th-thing when a man can't b-beat up his own b-b-b-boy!" Mick said, aggrieved. But he stopped shouting. He didn't, however, loosen his grip on Snotty.

"I'm NOT his boy!" Snotty howled. All he got for that was a slap across the face.

"Don't sh-sh-shout while the officer's t-t-talking. It's r-r-r-rude."

"Okay, let the boy go," Alan said.

"Sure, sure, sh-shure," Mick muttered. Reluctantly releasing his hold, he stood up and dusted off his trousers in an ingratiating way, just to show there were no hard feelings between him and the police.

Snotty's eyes snaked back and forth, looking for the best way out, while Mick pretended to search through his pockets for his i.d.

"I know it's here somewhere..."

Snotty started to inch backward. But a hand clamped down on his shoulder. "Oh, no you don't," Terry said, coming up from behind.

Snotty was in a jam, of that there was no doubt. The only good thing was that his money was still buried in the skip. Other than that, he couldn't think of a good word to say about the whole scenario.

But Snotty was, at bottom, a true entrepreneur. And your real entrepreneur knows that you're never out until they've put you in a cell and thrown away the key. Snotty knew he had a ways to go till then—only not very far.

The Dog saved him. An ominous growl came from the Seventh Garden, and when the others looked up, startled, it leapt out, teeth bared, a whirling mass of black and gray. Mick screamed and staggered back, while a startled Terry let his grip loose just enough so Snotty could yank away and run. With Alan on one side, and Terry on the other, he had no choice, really. It was the Seventh Garden for him. That or jail.

"Just get to the other side, over the fence, onto Hamercy Street,"

It was the Seventh Garden for him. That or jail.

he thought, running. The Dog ran by his side. "Almost there, almost there, we're out of here, yeah!" But his luck gave out. When Snotty (with the Dog following him) jumped onto the springy weeds at the center of the Seventh Garden, he felt them buckle and give. He skidded and froze, but it was too late for any of that. The weeds bounced and then gave way entirely. And with a faint 'plop,' Snotty and the Dog disappeared.

The next thing Snotty knew, he was falling. He grabbed hold of a weedy vine that stretched taut, but it broke. Then he tumbled down a hole. He felt the Dog leap past him as he fell straight into the darkness underneath.

Snotty fell and he fell and he fell. He fell past other smells he didn't know. Cedars on a hot day. Mushrooms frying in butter. Seaweed floating in a blue-green cove.[22]

He fell and he fell. Once he heard the dog howl, and then he thought that he could see stars above him. "Which makes no sense at all!" he thought. It had been many years since you could see stars in Megalopolis.[23]

Then he blacked out. Though he kept falling, he didn't, for a time, see or hear or feel anything more.

———————————

"Where is he?" Terry said wildly. Mick lay groaning in the dirt, clutching a torn pant leg where the Dog had stuck its teeth.

"He went into that garden," Alan said. "He'll be long gone by now."

"What garden?" Terry said.

And when Alan looked, there was no garden there.[24]

---

22   Common Arcadian motif. See above, note 20.

23   This, I believe, is still true. It certainly was in my childhood.

24   Dogs frequently figure as saviors/messengers in Arcadian stories. (See Bender

Chapter IV

DOWN THE RABBIT HOLE

"Drip...drip...drip...drip...."

"Snnnuuurrrgggghhh...."

"Drip...drip...drip...."

"Snoarrrgggghhh...."

Snotty lay on his back, eyes closed tight. His nose twitched. The air smelled damp and moldy. His head hurt.

"SSNNNARRRGGGGHHH?"

Something lay heavy on his stomach. It was making grunting noises, and its breath spread, warm and smelly, on Snotty's face.

He opened one eye. This made his head hurt worse—a piercing throb through his temples. The light was dim, but he could just make out the source of the grunting: the Dog, its gray and black snout lying across his chest. When the Dog saw Snotty was awake, it lifted its head and placed its paw on Snotty's arm.

Snotty groaned. Water dripped down the rock walls behind him and ran in rivulets down his collar. The Dog's brown eyes looked at

---

Boyce-Flood, year 25.) However, this is an uncommon motif in Megalopolitan tales. Prof. Bender Boyce-Flood has pointed out that many of the formerly autonomous communities swallowed up by Megalopolis have a tradition of stories of dogs acting as saviors from an oppressor. This is true of Arcadian tales as well. The most famous of these, of course, is "Dandy Drives the Devil Out," also the basis of a popular children's game, where a noble black dog can smell the Devil anywhere in Arcadia, and, finding him, jumps up, licking his face and pawing his fine clothes, smearing them with mud, until he retreats over the mountains back to Megalopolis. Professor Grayling has singled out the Dandy stories in his recent Censorship Edict affecting all Arcadian libraries.

him, and its nose prodded his face.

"Hey!" Snotty said weakly. "Don't!" He tried to lift his head up, had one dizzy impression of slate gray walls and damp moss, when another sharp pain went through his head, and he blacked out again.

———————

When he woke up the second time, he was alone.

———————

"Hello?" he said. He sat up again. His head still hurt, and the water running down his back had filled a puddle in his shirt that now ran down his jeans. He jumped up, shaking it out of his legs. He grimaced at the pain that shot through the back of his eyes, shook his head, and blinked, then looked around.

"It's a cave, I guess. I've fallen into a cave." This was reasonable enough, and comforted him as an explanation, though of course he couldn't for the life of him figure out what cave or where or why. He'd never been in a cave, though he'd seen them on TV. For now, though, he was happy to be able to say where he was at all.

"A cave. Definitely a cave. Okay. Good."

Now what?

He craned his neck and looked up from where he'd fallen. Up and up and up and up and up, he could see at the very top a tiny patch of cold gray sky. Daylight. He'd been lying here a long time.

"Drip...drip...drip...."

Foul smelling water dripped down the tangle of torn vines and branches that must have stopped his fall.

"Lucky, huh?" he said in a cheerful voice, and winced again at the pain in his head. Then he remembered the Dog. He looked around. "Dog," he said. "You there?" He gave a hopeful whistle. "Here, boy.

Here, boy." And he blinked again as his eyes got accustomed to the dim light.

He could see the source of that light now, at the end of a long tunnel. He had to squat down to look into it, the passage was so short and narrow—just big enough for a small boy to crawl through.

Snotty shrugged, got down on his hands and knees, and crawled.

The tunnel was shorter than it looked. As Snotty crawled, the light got brighter and golder, and he felt a little of its warmth. There were some ferns growing across the tunnel's outside face, blocking it. He pushed them out of the way, and the sun blazed inside. Snotty, startled, would have jumped backward, except he was hemmed in. To go forward, he had to scrabble and dig at the sides of the tunnel. After about ten minutes' effort, he widened it just enough so that he could wiggle through. On the other side, he straightened up and dusted himself off.

The first thing he noticed was the Silence. The sounds of the great city Megalopolis had completely disappeared. In place of them were the singing of birds and the rustling of leaves in a breeze. Except for these, it all was pretty quiet. Certainly quieter than anything Snotty was used to.

This made him nervous.

Trying to get his bearings, he saw he stood on a green hillside. This was covered with soft grass and wildflowers of white and purple and yellow—a much different landscape than the one he was used to. His eyes narrowed suspiciously as he looked around. The mountain he'd crawled out of was at his back, and this was taller than the hills rolling away from him on three sides. At their foot was a long broad plain that spread out until it reached an even taller mountain range, far away.

"Great," Snotty sighed. "Nature. Swell."

Snotty knew Nature when he saw it, of course, having learned about mountains and rivers and oceans and those kinds of things in his school's lone science class—at least, until he stopped going. Nature hadn't interested him much. He couldn't see the use of it.[25]

"Still, it's something new, right?" he said to himself, cheering up. "Maybe it'll be a laugh. An adventure, anyway." At that thought, Snotty's little red eyes gleamed. He liked adventures, no matter what kind. And this was one of the nicest things about him—although it's true there wasn't much in the way of competition.

So, set for adventure, Snotty checked out the landscape.

The rolling hills themselves he dismissed. "Boring," he commented briefly, looking skeptically at their tufts of green and bursts of flower. Near their bottom, though, was a more rugged bit, gray and brown and rocky.

"That looks kind of interesting," he admitted to himself.

He couldn't quite make out what happened past that, even though he squinted and shaded his eyes against an unfamiliar sun. There seemed to be a band of dark green, maybe a strip of trees or something, then beyond that a mix of green and brown and black. There were a lot of bright red and black things moving around there— from up here they looked like beetles. But he didn't worry about that now. Just past that, though, was something more interesting: a camp, or a fairground, covered with lots of tents and flags, all red and purple and gold and emerald green.

Snotty liked that. Tents meant people, and people meant business

---

25   I can attest to this being a common feeling among Megalopolitan students, at least in my youth! In science classes held at Megalopolis's Technical Academy for the Betterment of Mankind, where I studied classical Megalopolitan physics, it was uncommon to study directly from nature. Abstract/generated models were thought to be more accurate. I now believe this to have been the result of Megalopolitan environmental degradation, which had made nature more difficult to study in its true form.

opportunities. Automatically, Snotty began to wonder which of his stories might play the best with an adult audience here. And he went on considering the view.

Beyond the camp was a yellow desert that spread out around the multicolored tents until it stopped at another row of foothills, which in their turn rose up into the farthest-off range of green and brown and white mountains. Down the sides of these mountains ran a tangle of creeks, streams, and rivers—water of all kinds—that either ran into a larger river below or stopped at the edge of the vast glowing desert.

Snotty wasn't much interested in any of that.

One thing did catch his eye: a triangular and pure white peak that stood up behind the mountains on the far horizon, the tallest and farthest and grandest of them all. As Snotty looked at this impressive sight, his mouth half open, a cloud rose up behind it and covered it in shadow. There was a far off rumble of thunder. "Hmm," he said. "That's the tallest thing there is around here." Snotty was impressed, as he always was with anything the biggest, the tallest, or the most grand. All Megalopolitans were like that, actually.

"But what I really need is some action," Snotty thought to himself. (All Megalopolitans liked action, too.) "And I'm not getting much of that just standing here, am I? So..."

Without worrying too much about what he would do when he got wherever it was, he started down the hill. It was, after all, the only way ahead.

———————

As he walked, though, he started to feel lonely. Now, Snotty was not used to feeling lonely, though he had always been very much alone, and so he didn't at first recognize this for what it was. "Head for those tents, that's my best bet," he thought, making his way down the boulder-strewn hill. "Bound to be money in a place like that."

As he went on, he considered what story he would tell the people he met about who he was and what he was doing there. These were obviously people who liked Nature, he thought with a grimace, so he tailored it to what he thought Nature-loving people would like. "My uncle, who's a marine biologist...no, marine, that's the ocean, right? My uncle, who's a BOTANIST, brought me...what do they call it? Camping, right. He brought me camping. And I got lost...and my uncle will be so worried...and he'll really want to reward anyone who takes care of me till he comes..." As he went on automatically spinning a new story to himself, he became aware of a vague pain in his chest. "Must've hurt myself when I fell," he reasoned, trying to ignore it. But as he went on, the pain got sharper and harsher. Soon it hurt so much that he had to stop and catch his breath.

This was Loneliness. But Snotty didn't recognize it. You might say that Snotty and Loneliness had never been formally introduced.

"What is it?" he thought, and he gasped as Loneliness stabbed him hard again. The very silence around him, broken only now and then by the calling of a lone bird, seemed to join with the pain and make it worse. "This really, really, really hurts," Snotty thought. He couldn't catch his breath. It seemed to Snotty that he couldn't breathe at all. As there was no one to see, Snotty sat back on the ground. He hugged his knees to his chest and pressed his forehead to his knees.

That was when he heard the Dog. "Grrrooowwfff!" it barked from far away, echoing up the hill. "Ggrroowwff."

At this, Snotty's breath came back in a rush, and he leapt up, looking around eagerly. "Hello?" he called out. "Dog? Where are you?"

"ggrroowf," the bark came back, fainter now, as the Dog moved away. "ggrof."

"Wait!" Snotty called. His voice echoed back to him. "Wait for me!" He scanned the landscape. Then he saw the Dog, a small black and gray splotch running farther down the hillside.

Snotty ran after it. But the Dog ran faster now, letting out a sharp bark, then a second. Snotty, tripping and falling and tumbling among the boulders dotting the hill, soon lost sight of it. "DON'T LEAVE ME!" he wailed, picking himself up and running forward, only to trip and fall again. Then there was silence, except for the sound of the bird. The Dog was gone.

Snotty bit his lip.

"I don't care," he said. "I always hated dogs anyway." That made him feel better, and he walked on.

He felt even better—well, more comfortable, anyway—when, as he walked (and this he did more and more slowly with every step), the beautiful landscape disappeared. Now he could see that gray and brown part of the landscape up close. It was mud. Just mud. Only mud. And lots of it, too.

The sight of all that mud cheered him up no end. It reminded him of home, which is always nice when you're far away from it.

There was lots of mud now. Snotty trudged across it. And the mud got muddier and muddier the farther he walked. It sucked at the bottom of his shoes, and before long it was up around his ankles, making squooshing noises.

He slogged on. But eventually he couldn't go any farther. The mud was halfway up his legs now, sucking at his knees.

From the far off distance came a dull noise. BOOM. BOOM. BOOM. This startled him, and he tried to go back the way he'd come. But he just stuck more firmly in the mud. It was up past his knees now—blackish and bad smelling. Every time Snotty heaved himself out, it heaved with him, covering more of his legs.

He was stuck.

"Okay," he muttered once he found he couldn't move an inch in any direction whatsoever, "enough's enough. A joke's a joke. Let me out of here, now!" He yanked hard with both arms at his left leg. At this, he lost his balance and fell into the mud face down.

"Bbbbllluurrrggghh?" he said. Then, "brrrarrrggggh?"

And then, his arms windmilling in the mud, "bbbbbrrrrraaaa-AAAAAGGGGGGGHHHH!" The more he thrashed about trying to get free, though, the deeper he dug himself in.

If it weren't for his big nose, which had pushed an air pocket in the mud, he would have smothered there for sure.

"Fine!" he thought to himself, thoroughly annoyed. "So this is Nature! Great! Swell! Yeah!" He bitterly remembered his science teacher boring the class on and on about Nature's glories. "I'd like to rub his face in this stuff just for..."

SSSLLLUUURRRRPPPPHHHHH! A Herculean effort on Snotty's part managed to set one ear free. "Not that there's anything to hear. Nothing but that stupid bird."

But even that stupid bird had flown away, apparently. And then there was no sound at all.

This was the worst of all. Snotty lay there tensely, waiting for he didn't know what.

Then, with his one free ear, he heard a voice.

"Excuse me," it said in a pleasant and unhurried way. "Can I help?"

Chapter V

SNOWFLAKE

There was a pause while Snotty considered this.

"Yyyyeeerrrrrgggghhh," he said, at last.

The voice considered this. "I'll take that as a yes," it finally said. And a nose—or something like a nose, anyway—snuffled at Snotty's back. Snotty screeched, which came out "bbbllluuuurrrgggghhh." Meanwhile the snuffly thing pushed here and there until it got a hold on Snotty's jeans. These it grabbed between its teeth and with a SSQQQUUUIRRRCCCCHH! yanked him up out of the mud hole, dragged him through the sludge and deposited him on a rocky path.

"There," the voice said in a pleased sort of way. "That's better."

Snotty gagged and spat out some muck. He sat up and, wiping the mud out of his eyes with his muddy forearm, looked at his rescuer.

This was a small white and silver horse.

Snotty blinked with surprise. The horse blinked back. It seemed just as surprised as he.

"Well," the horse said. "Not what I expected at all!"

But then Snotty, to his great relief, recognized the little horse.

"I KNOW you!" he said, jumping up and down on the rocky path in his excitement. "You're a PONY! I RODE you. At a funfair. I snuck in without paying. You had a saddle and a saddlebag and everything. And your name on the saddlebag. It was...it was...it was..." Snotty snapped his fingers together, trying to remember.

"Snowflake?" suggested the horse.

"That's right!" Snotty said. "Snowflake! Exactly! But what are you doing here?"

"I remember, too," Snowflake reminisced, nudging Snotty with his muzzle. They started down the path together. "You kicked me when no one was looking."

Snotty looked ashamed. It was true. He had kicked Snowflake. But somebody had been looking–that was the whole point. Stan and the boys, sneaking into the fair after him, had stood there jeering at him for enjoying himself. Snotty had to do something. Anyone could have seen that.

"I didn't want to kick you, exactly." He tried to explain himself but it came out all garbled. "Besides," he said, trying again, "I knew you wouldn't mind, being so much more mature than them, and all." But this sounded too whiny and wheedly, even to him. Finally, he gave up.

"Well, never mind," Snowflake said.

"Anyway," Snotty said lamely, "I'm glad to see you again." But Snowflake didn't answer and Snotty followed him in silence down a particularly steep and rocky stretch of the path. Snotty skidded once, right at the bottom, but Snowflake offered his shoulder, and Snotty steadied himself. That was when he saw the wound between the little horse's eyes.

It wasn't so much of a wound as a scar that hadn't healed right. It was scraped red and raw in the center, and glittered with silver around the edge.

"What happened to your head?" Snotty said, interested. Snowflake looked unhappy at the question and didn't answer. His green eyes searched Snotty's face.

"Don't you remember?" Snowflake said.

"What?" Snotty asked, astonished. "What do you mean?" Did Snowflake mean it had happened at the fair?

But instead of answering, the little horse turned away.

Puzzled, Snotty kept walking. They were on level ground now, where the path curved through another grassy meadow. Up ahead was a huge black wrought iron gate.

From the distance came that sound again. BOOM. BOOM. BOOM.

"What's that?"

"Have you forgotten that, too?" Snowflake said in his gentle way. Then he broke into a trot.

"Look," Snotty said, running to catch up. "I don't know what you're talking about. You must have the wrong boy. You..."

They neared the gate. It was an old thing, rusting and spiked, but it was held shut by a shining new chain.

"Sssssh," Snowflake said. "Not now." The little horse stared at the gate, his eyes narrowed.

Leaning up against the fence was a placard, with writing so new that Snotty could smell the paint. It said:

THE GARDEN OF EARTHLY DELIGHTS
> No Nymphs
> No Devas
> No Angels
> No Sprites/Fairies/Pixies
> Absolutely NO Unicorns[26]

---

26   All creatures recently proven to exist, though much still needs to be done to determine where and how. (See Dr. Alan Fallaize, *On the Discovery of Biological Truths in Fairy Tales*, Otterbridge University Press, year 61.) Even Professor Grayling agrees, though he and the Neofundamentalists are violently opposed to allowing any of these creatures into Councils of Arcadian State. One of the causes of the present civil war was our late queen's wish that an Angel be installed as a minister. This suggestion was met by an immediate outbreak of arbitrary violence meant to stop the program of reform started by Lily the Silent, and continued by Sophia the Wise. Her ministers, of which I am one, struggled against the escalation of these terrorist attacks into a full civil war. But in vain.

Please stay on the path at all times.
Thank you, the NEW MANAGEMENT

"Two singles, please," Snotty heard Snowflake say in his patient voice. (He wondered what a Deva was, but he didn't like to ask.) A yellow Sheep with red-rimmed eyes peered out at them from a ticket booth.

"Mmmmmaaaaaaaa?" it said suspiciously.

Snowflake gave an indifferent shrug. "As you see," he said.

The Sheep stared at Snotty. "Bah," it said. But the little horse ignored this.

As they passed, the Sheep glared at them.

"I don't like the way he's looking at me," Snotty muttered.

"Ignore him," Snowflake said.

Instead, Snotty glared back at the Sheep. But the Sheep wasn't looking at him, it was looking at Snowflake, and it clearly didn't like what it saw. As they walked through the turnstile into the Garden, though, Snotty forgot all about that, and concentrated, as he always did, on what was ahead of him, instead of on what was behind.

Chapter VI
ALADDIN'S TREASURE

The Garden of Earthly Delights wasn't much to look at. It had been torn up recently, trees and flowers and plants tossed here and there, yellowish brown and dying. And there was nothing yet planted in their place.

"Not much of a garden, is it?" Snotty said. At this, Snowflake only looked sad and nudged him forward, toward the edge of an enormous lawn that stretched out as far as the eye could see.

This was a remarkable lawn. It was even and green and each one of its individual blades was uniform in size and color. It was soft like velvet and expensive as all get out. There was not one weed—not a dandelion, not a clover flower, not a piece of plantain. Nothing but lush green grass. And it was brand new.

"This is more like it!" Snotty said. "This is more what a Garden of Earthly Delights should be!" And now he could see who made the Garden the way it was. A dozen Giant Garden Gnomes, in bright red jackets and black leather boots, tended it, rooting up everything that wasn't lawn and tossing it aside.

Snotty approved. "If you've got a lawn like that," he thought enthusiastically, "you want to keep it looking great in every way." So he admired the Gnomes' work. But he was also uneasy remembering his last encounter with a Garden Gnome, and, just in case his behavior toward that little Gnome might be misunderstood by these, its much larger fellows, he thought it might be best to admire their work from afar. So without another word he walked quickly in another direction, leaving Snowflake behind.

The sound of digging caught his attention, and he saw a Sheep burying things stacked high on a wheelbarrow. As he drew closer, he could see what these things were: old china dolls, pieces of colored quilts, broken arrows, pressed flowers and a French horn. He stood for a while watching the Sheep shovel these into a deep hole in the lawn.

The sight was so engrossing that he didn't notice, behind him, two Giant Garden Gnomes march on Snowflake and demand of him something or other, to which the little horse, in his meek way, assented. Neither did Snotty see the Garden Gnomes peer at Snowflake's head and then put a rope around his neck, leading him away. He didn't even notice his friend was gone.

Instead he watched the Sheep. He saw there was a method to the way the Sheep buried things. It would spread a layer of them—a white and green glass bracelet, an amateur seascape, and a rocking horse—at the bottom of the pit, then shovel in more dirt before spreading another layer—this time a bouquet of dried white flowers tied with yellowing satin ribbons, three dead kittens, and a gold metal tree hung with bells—on top. And so on.

"Hey," Snotty said. "Fantastic lawn."

The Sheep grunted but, flattered by Snotty's interest, handed him the shovel and let him wield it for a while. Snotty pushed a pile of jack-in-the-boxes and piñatas into the pit.[27]

"Mmmmaaaaaa!" the Sheep protested, by which Snotty understood it to mean that this was not the right way.

Snotty blinked. "You're kidding, right?" he said.

---

27   It was this section describing the lawn and its composition that was one of the missing chapters of the *Legendus Snottianicus*, only to be discovered when the copy of *Snotty Saves the Day* was found in Queen Sophia's library after her death. As such, it deserves much closer study. (See Vale, *The Legendus Snottianicus: The More We Know, the Less We Understand*, Otterbridge University Press, year 54, for this history.) It is worth noting that the only form of nature valued in Megalopolis is the lawn.

"Bbbbaaaaa!" the Sheep said, snatching the shovel back. After that there didn't seem to be much to say, so, shrugging his shoulders, Snotty walked on.

He was alone again, but he didn't feel so bad about that now. He had forgotten Snowflake. But he did remember he was hungry. Hurrying across the lawn, he looked around for a place to get something to eat. At the end of the lawn were the multicolored tents he'd seen from above. And he'd been right: they were a marketplace, a bazaar, a fair. This was something Snotty was very familiar with from home, and he headed toward it with a renewed sense of confidence and expectation. He was not disappointed.

It was very satisfying for a fair. For example, there were the sounds. Shrill hawkers called out the beauties of their wares. Then there were the sights. Ruby, emerald, and sapphire colored silks; gold and silver, both in chunks as big as a baby's head and also worked. There were filigree birdcages containing silver birds, lanterns, workboxes, graceful platters, and wide hammered bowls. There were the smells. Snotty, remembering how hungry he was, followed his nose.[28] There were aisles of brass bowls filled with hot roasted nuts. There were bright colored hard candies and slabs of chocolate with edges melting in the sun. There were skewered birds roasting on open braziers, black marks caramelizing on their breasts. Brown and gold chunks of smoked fish. Vats of popcorn weighed down with melted butter. Fountains of soda.

Snotty didn't waste time. He stole the first piece of food he could, a bright red candied apple, and wolfed it down. The vendor, an angry-looking Sheep, turned just in time to see the last bit disappear down Snotty's gullet, and gave a shout. But Snotty disappeared, quick as a rat, under a table covered with salt-water taffy and nut brittle. He was well away before he could be caught.

As he scurried along under the tables, he snatched, here and

---

28   See above notes on motif of smells, good and bad.

there, a sausage, a bag of sugared almonds, and a hunk of bright orange cheese. Hiding these under his shirt, he darted in and out of the aisles looking for a place to enjoy them undisturbed. He found one on the far side of the Bazaar, at the back of the tents, next to the overflowing trash barrels where what wasn't sold was thrown out. It was here that Snotty settled, sitting with a wary back to the garbage heaps, and here he ate the sausage and cheese in alternate bites. He finished with a dessert of the violently colored candied nuts.

"This is a nice quiet spot," Snotty thought. Then he burped. "Maybe I'll take a little nap."

But it was not to be, that nap.

"PPPSSSSSTTTT."

Snotty, who had thought he was alone, gave a jump and looked around.

"Psssttt," the sound repeated. "Hey, kid! Yeah, you! I'm talking to you!"

There, right in front of Snotty, was a young and beautiful man. He stood there, holding open the folds of a topaz colored tent, as if he'd been there all along. He had gold and bronze hair that shone like metal, parted in a sharp line down one side. He had white skin and turquoise blue eyes. When he stepped out from behind the tent, Snotty could see that he wore a smoking jacket with a foulard tie, and on his feet were a pair of golden slippers with turned-up toes.

"Help me out, kid," the beautiful young man pleaded in a nervous undertone. He twitched as he spoke, scratching his nose and sniffling. "I've got to move some treasure, cheap. It's an emergency. Come on. You're in the right place at the right time. You'll never see a price like this again. And the merchandise?" The beautiful young man kissed his fingertips. "Sweet."

Snotty just stared.

When Snotty made no move, the beautiful young man held up one finger. "Oh, yeah. You don't know me. You need some bona fides. No problem. Wait here." And he disappeared back into the tent.

Snotty waited with interest for what would happen next.

A moment later, the beautiful young man reappeared. This time he held a sign. "Me," he said, pointing.

The sign said: "ALADDIN'S CAVE. TREASURE BOUGHT AND SOLD. NO PRICE FIRM. NO OFFER IGNORED."

"So?" Snotty said. He was curious, though he was careful not to let Aladdin see this.

"Well," Aladdin said. "You interested or what? Make up your mind. I'm in a hurry for a sale." And the beautiful young man's turned-up left toes tapped a nervous tattoo in the dust.

Snotty was on firm ground now. He'd negotiated enough deals in his time to know when he had the advantage. This guy was clearly desperate.

He considered Aladdin, gave a terse nod, and followed him to the other side of the amber silk wall.

It really was an Aladdin's Cave. The gold! The jewels! The old paintings! All were scattered across an Oriental carpeted floor in careless heaps, glowing in the shadows of the tent. Snotty's eyes widened in spite of himself, and he turned away to hide the fact that he was impressed.

"Humph," he grunted. "What a lot of stuff."

"I got it from a couple of genies," Aladdin said in a quick undertone, his tongue flicking out to lick his dry lips. His nose was running, and he wiped it on the burgundy velvet sleeve of his jacket. "It's hot, you understand. I've got to get rid of it. Cheap."

Snotty, looking bored, fingered a piece of gold brocade. "How much?" he said, suppressing a yawn.

Aladdin drew in his breath along with some smoke from a spicy-smelling cigarette. "An arm and a leg takes the whole lot," he said in a terse voice, and with an exhale sent the cigarette's smoke back into

It really was an Aladdin's Cave. The gold! The jewels!

the room.

Snotty coughed at the smoke and waved it away. He couldn't believe his luck. Aladdin didn't want cash for his treasure. Just body parts. A quick look around told Snotty what the treasure was worth on the open market. A lot more than an arm and a leg. That gold and crystal lamp on the ebony stand there, that alone was worth at least an elbow.

Snotty was filled with confidence now. He had done this kind of deal before, and he knew how to play it. Giving a scornful snort, he let Aladdin know how ridiculous he considered the price. He shook his head and turned to leave.

And then, just as he had reckoned, Aladdin grabbed his shirt and pulled him back.

With an intent look, he said, "Too rich for you?" Snotty yawned outright this time. "So bargain," the beautiful young man said, trying, to Snotty's delight, to keep the pleading tone out of his voice. "I'm motivated."

Snotty yawned again, very bored. "Well," he said skeptically. "How much for an eye."

Aladdin looked worried. "Half," he said fast. Too fast. Snotty had his measure now. He was sure of it.

"Still too much," Snotty said to Aladdin. He turned away again. But then at the last minute he turned back, as if with a second thought.

"A little finger," he offered. And his expression showed this was his final offer.

"You're killing me," Aladdin complained. But when Snotty turned away for a third time, and Aladdin said, "Right or left?", Snotty knew he had him.

They agreed on his right little finger, as long as Aladdin threw in that ebony lamp stand with all the rest. Snotty held out his hand to pay, and the beautiful young man pulled out a jeweled chainsaw and started it up.

After the deal was done, outside Aladdin's tent and back in the thick of the Bazaar, Snotty considered what to do next. He had bargained hard and gotten Aladdin to throw in a piece of that gold brocade with which to wrap the treasure. A small torn off bit of it bandaged the throbbing stump that had been his little finger. Its stiff gold threads rubbed in an uncomfortable way against the wound.[29]

"That kind of hurts," he thought vaguely. "I wonder if I could get some ice for it somewhere." Looking around, he saw he was being stared at, hard, by a Sheep selling kebabs by the skewer from a sizzling grill.

"Hey," Snotty said, "Excuse me." He held up his hand. "You got anything I could put on this?" But the Sheep didn't answer. It just stared at him harder. Another Sheep joined him. They both stared.

Snotty, unnerved by this, pretended an interest in the wares in front of him on a table. "What's that?" he said, pointing at a stack of tapering ivory wands.

"Unicorn horns," the second Sheep said in a short voice. It kept its sullen eyes on Snotty while the first Sheep produced a furled piece of poster. He opened this and the two sheep studied it, looking up from time to time toward Snotty.

This made Snotty uneasy.

Clutching his bag of treasure to his chest, he backed down the aisle the way he had come. "I don't know what's up," he thought. "But whatever it is, I don't like it." All around him now, in the Bazaar, he could see sheep of all kinds staring at him. Each one held a piece of unfurled paper.

"It's HIM!" a voice squeaked. A fluffy little Lambkin glared up at Snotty from under a table. At its feet was a WANTED poster, and

---

29   The motif of the hero mutilating him/herself for illusory advantage is a common one in Arcadian fairy tales. It is also common in Megalopolitan folk tales, though here the hero is considered to have behaved in a manly, as opposed to the Arcadian naïve, fashion. The difference is salutary.

on the WANTED poster was Snotty's face. When Snotty, startled, looked up, he saw there were posters everywhere, hung from every tent post saying the same thing. WANTED: SNOTTY. Snotty didn't need to see any more. He turned and hurried as fast as he could back to the end of the aisle, hampered though he was with his clanking bag of treasure. He pushed his way through the thin amethyst colored silk of the tent there only to find, on the other side, three Giant Garden Gnomes waiting for him. They were dressed in red coats with shining silver buttons, and shiny black leather boots. They had green cocked hats and long white beards. And they were mounted on tall rocking horses, sabers at the ready.

"This looks bad," Snotty thought, anxiously remembering his last encounter with a Garden Gnome. "But let's wait a sec. Maybe I'm just being paranoid. Maybe...."

The Largest Giant Garden Gnome bellowed through a bullhorn.

"ATTENTION, SNOTTY! COME OUT WITH YOUR HANDS UP! THERE IS NO ESCAPE! RESISTANCE IS FUTILE!"

"Oh-oh," gulped Snotty, clutching his treasure even tighter now. A quick look around confirmed the worst. Sheep and Gnomes surrounded him on all sides.

Snotty's instinct for survival, always strong, took over now. "No!" he shouted. "Wait! I got TREASURE! I can BRIBE you guys!" With that, he threw the treasure on the ground in hopes of making the most impressive display he could.

The Gnomes, the Sheep, and Snotty all craned their necks looking down at the dirt. As the bag broke open, a pile of grayish dust, some broken glass, and seven cockroaches spilled out. The cockroaches ran off right away. There was silence as all stared at what was left of the pile of trash.[30]

---

30 Treasure turning to trash is so common a motif in Arcadian folk tales that any Arcadian child could name you twenty stories revolving around the transformation. There are no known instances of the same transformation in any Megalopolitan

Snotty, furious, gave a yell.

"I was ROBBED!" He stamped his foot so hard on the ground that the one last beetle left in the bag leapt out and scurried away.

The Gnomes laughed at the sight of the maimed and cheated Snotty storming in circles, yowling with frustration and rage—especially when his bandage fell off, and his stump began to bleed. "That," the Largest Giant Garden Gnome commented, "is very funny." The other Gnomes agreed. So they were in a fine mood as they lassoed our hero and dragged him through the desert dust to a jail dug into the side of a small hill.

Snotty, coughing, tried not to swallow too much dirt as he was dragged along, but in this he didn't much succeed. The Largest Giant Garden Gnome dismounted from his rocking horse and, seeing Snotty's expression, gave a chuckle as if at a very good joke, then unlocked the jail door and shoved Snotty inside. The door shut with a dull thud, and Snotty could hear the scrape and thump of a thick plank being put in place to bar him inside.

---

stories that I can find. (See Vale, year 22; Vale, year 26.) The most common Arcadian motif involves three sisters, one after another going over the mountains in search of a husband. Halfway there, and offered a choice between a mansion filled with splendid clothes, or a half-starved dog, the first two sisters choose the mansion only to be left with a small pile of brown pellets. The third sister, inevitably moved by compassion, chooses the dog, only to have him turn into a handsome prince. The famous Arcadian Maude stories also begin this way, with Maude marrying her dog husband before going on to further adventures.

Chapter VII
SNOTTY THE SUN GOD[31]

It was pitch black in the jail. Time passed slowly. Snotty's wound throbbed and so did his head. But there was nothing to do but wait.

Another hour passed. The jail was hot and close. Snotty dozed, uneasy and mad.

Then, from far away, came the sound of a bugle.

"Tooo-tttooootooootoooo-tooooo..."

Then the sound of a thousand marching feet.

Then the sound of a military band.

"Huh? What's that?" Snotty jerked awake. The marching feet came closer and closer, until they stopped right outside the barred jail door. Snotty heard the scraping and bumping of the large plank. The door opened.

Snotty clenched his teeth and his fists and waited for what came next.

But nothing came next. Light streamed in the door from outside. No one appeared to drag Snotty away. All was silent now, except for

---

31 The Sun God is an important motif in all worlds existing under suns. A fruitful area for study, especially since initial research proves that stories of a Sun God's triumphs are common to dominator/hierarchical societies such as Megalopolis. This is the only known instance of a Sun God motif in all of Arcadian literature, with the exception of the fraudulent Siegfried Cycle, written anonymously by Professor Grayling as propaganda for what Neofundamentalists call "The New Man," who (they claim) is the proper ruler of Arcadia. (See Prof. Aspern Grayling, editor, *The Siegfried Cycle*, New Power Press, year 43.)

the moan of the desert wind—and, in the distance, the tinny sound of the band.

"Present ARMS!" a far-off voice called. And there was the sound of the click of a thousand swords against metal.

Curious now—but with his fists still clenched—Snotty stepped into the doorway and blinked in the light.

Outside a double line of Gnomes faced each other at attention. The arms they presented clicked against the shiny buttons of their military coats.

A voice barked behind Snotty, making him jump.

"SIR!" it shouted. "Your horse is ready, SIR!"

Sure enough, at the end of the long corridor of standing-at-attention Gnomes stood a large white rocking horse.

Snotty began a cautious walk through the lines. On either side of him, Giant Garden Gnomes stood five deep. Those not presenting arms saluted as he passed.

He saluted back.

When he reached the rocking horse—a high-spirited stallion held by an orderly—he saw a tailor's dummy beside it. On the dummy was a navy blue and red military coat, rich with medals, and a large hat trimmed with a matching cockade. Snotty stripped off his torn shirt and put these on. A perfect fit. The Orderly Gnome held out his hands to help Snotty into the saddle. Snotty sprang up onto his stallion, and the Orderly handed him his sword.

Looking out over the heads of the rigid troops, Snotty saw the three Giant Garden Gnomes who had captured him quailing before a red-faced, white-haired General. "You idiots!" yelled the General Gnome, shaking a furled poster in their faces. "Nincompoops! Nitwits! Numbskulls! Ignoramuses and Fatheads!" Then the General Gnome turned from them in disgust and galloped on his own magnificent steed of red and black toward Snotty. As he approached, Snotty, with a newly formed honor guard of mounted Gnomes, rode up a straight

"SNOTTY THE SUN GOD! HOORAY!"

road to the top of a butte.

It seemed to Snotty, more confident with each moment that passed, that he knew just how to behave. The crest of the butte sparkled gold in the desert sun. He rode for this, his guard following. The General brought up the rear. The white stallion rocking horse kept up a steady gait. Snotty was pleased to find that he knew how to ride a rocking horse.

"But then," he thought, "I have always known that I was a Great Man."[32]

Each moment that passed confirmed him in this view. As he rode, sheep strewed rose petals in his path, bowing their woolly heads and filling the air with their baaas. Snotty rode to the edge of the butte, the light of the sun behind him. Below him, thousands and thousands of Giant Garden Gnomes stood at attention.

Snotty raised his sword high. The sunlight glittered off its blade. The Gnomes yelled, their giant fists in the air. Snotty could just make out these words: "SNOTTY THE SUN GOD! SNOTTY THE SUN GOD! HOORAY!"

Snotty, pleased at being the center of attention, took this new development in stride. In fact, as he waved his sword at the adoring masses, he felt just the tiniest bit bummed. If it was inevitable that his greatness should one day shine on the world stage, he thought it might have happened sooner.

But a Great Man is always ready to Forget the Past and Greet the

---

32   The Great Man motif has been definitively analyzed by Dr. Malcolm Sivia in his classic *Connection: A Personal Journey of Discovery, Loss, and Love*, Otterbridge University Press, year 59. This work is an essential research tool for any student of Arcadian fairy and folk tales, as well as of physics and biology, and theorizes a difference between societies that admire single transcendent culture heroes, and those that have as models twins, brother/sister combinations, or married couples. Again, this marks a well-known split in Arcadian thought. See Grayling, year 43, for the single example in Arcadian literature of the Great Man saving society.

New Day, so Snotty sat, straight and genial in the saddle, his expression an abstracted smile—as if his head were too full of great plans for him to take much notice of anything else. The Gnomes below continued their shouts, and Snotty experimented with turning first this way, then that, and letting the sun glint not just off his sword, but off the shiny buttons of his coat as well.

The white-haired General Gnome rode up to him and presented arms.

"Sorry about that before, sir," the General said. "Those blockheads mistook you for a common criminal. They had no idea you were Snotty the Sun God."[33]

Now Snotty was not at all sure what a Sun God was. Still he had a shrewd idea that it was something fairly high up the Christmas tree.

Snotty waved a small hand in a gesture of disdain, as if to say that such petty matters were best soon forgot. This was the attitude, he felt, that should accompany Greatness. Admiring looks passed among the Gnomes of his entourage, so he was probably right.

"Sir," the General Gnome said. "We must repair to your fortress. And to the Grand Feast."

"We must," Snotty agreed, careful to keep his expression as lofty as he could.

"But first," the General Gnome continued, "the tradition of the GREAT PARDON."

Snotty gave a grave nod, although of course he had no idea what the Great Pardon could be.

The General Gnome addressed the troops below. "Fellow Gnomes!" he boomed. "As was foretold, our Sun God has returned to us! It is written in the Gnomic Book of Deeds: 'HE WILL COME AMONG US AND WE WILL KNOW HIM. FOR HE WILL SACRIFICE HIS VERY FINGER FOR A MESS OF TRASH!'" At this he grabbed Snotty's hand and held it up to the sun, which shone

---

33　See Sivia, above note 32.

through the space where his littlest finger had once been.[34]

The crowd went wild. The Gnomes whooped and hollered and threw their Gnome hats into the air. They chanted, "SNOTTY. SNOTTY. SNOTTY."

But the General Gnome held up a hand. There was an expectant silence. "And now," he boomed, "as is our tradition, the Sun God will grant a merciful pardon to OUR CHOICE OF MONSTER!"

Snotty shifted uneasily. He didn't like the sound of the word 'monster,' but he kept his expression as blank as he could. The band struck up a doleful tune. And from the ranks of the Gnomes came a line of prisoners, chained together and sobbing and crying for mercy. All, that is, but one.

There were five in all. The first was a fire-breathing Pig, with stiff iron bristles on its chin. The second was a Monstrous Woman, taller than the largest Gnome, her hair and talons streaked with red and white. The third was a silver Bear. The fourth was a Dragon with a bat's wings and a lion's head.

All these four moaned and pleaded. "Wow," Snotty said to the General Gnome. "Cool." The General Gnome nodded, pleased.

The fifth prisoner alone was quiet, hiding behind the others. A Gnome Guard gave it a vicious kick that forced it forward. Only then did Snotty see that the fifth prisoner was Snowflake.

What a wretched thing Snowflake was in that company! The little horse was dull-eyed and beaten; its head dragged in the dust, its pelt was matted and gray, and its hooves were cracked. The crowd greeted it with jeers.

The Dragon was clearly the favorite. And no wonder. Its scales

---

34 This motif of the missing finger is rare in Arcadian literature, but when found there indicates a chosen one of some kind. Our late queen, Lily the Silent, mother of Sophia the Wise, by coincidence, was missing just such a finger. I have had occasion to question her as to the circumstances in which she lost the digit, but in this, as in so much else, our dear queen lived up to her name.

shone like those of a fish jumping in a mountain lake. Its wings were as wide as the butte, their color a translucent black. In its lion's head, its eyes shone a deep turquoise blue.

"I am the Dragon!" it roared. Its brilliant eyes stared straight at Snotty, reminding him of something, even if he couldn't remember what. "I serve he who has the courage to sell his finger for a mess of trash!"[35]

"That's the GNOME WAY!" shouted someone in the ranks. "You tell 'em!" And the Gnomes again shouted and hollered and threw their hats in the air.

After that, the display of the other monsters was an anticlimax. The Woman disdained to play to the crowd. The Bear tried without success to compete with the Dragon. The Pig's flames had gone out, even though it tried hard to get them going again. Now it couldn't manage anything but a grunt.

Snowflake, head bowed, just stood there in his quiet way.

"The DRAGON!" the crowd cried as the monsters, chains

---

35   Again, I am indebted to Prof. Grayling for insights regarding the Dragon, to be published in a separate monograph of mine provisionally entitled *Lives of Things That Go Bump in the Night: A Meditation on Dreams and Their Dreamers*. My thesis, of course, is that a Dreamer is in partnership with her/his Dreams, and may, on occasion, bring them to life. The question remains as to whether the Dreams preexist the Dreamer. Are the Dreams already existent in another world? Or does the Dreamer create the Dreams? Professor Grayling and I, in the days before he reinvented himself as *éminence grise* of the Neofundamentalist side of our Civil War, held many a spirited discussion on this subject. Dragons were a case in point. Professor Grayling was known for the small, fierce Dragon he kept as a pet—the only one in Arcadia. He asserted his will had created the Dragon. But research has shown that, at certain points, other worlds intersect with ours. We have, for example, been able to access libraries in a world that seems to exist simultaneously with ours, and in the same space. (Dr. Alan Fallaize has continued experiments to contact people in this world, as well, so far discovering that it is possible to convey folk and fairy tales.) It is possible that Dragons do exist, and that Grayling, instead of creating his pet, worked to bring it into our world from another.

clanking, made their way toward Snotty. "The Dragon! Free the DRAGON!"

Even though Snotty hadn't been a Sun God for very long, he knew enough not to go against a crowd. Anyway, he liked that Dragon, too. It was big. It was cool. It was definitely grand.

So impressed was Snotty, in fact, that he forgot all about Snowflake.

With a lordly gesture, he uncurled one hand toward the Dragon. A great cheer came from the troops as the guards released the monster from its chains.

The Dragon roared; its wings flapped. It flew straight to Snotty, where it bent one reptilian knee, demonstrating its loyalty to the Sun God.

At this Snotty gave a modest grin.

Cheers rang out. Drunk with success, Snotty wheeled his horse around and rode beside the General off the butte. The Dragon and the Guard of Honor followed close behind.

As they trotted on their noble rocking horses toward the Grand Feast, Snotty said, "By the way, General. Those other monsters, the ones I didn't free: what happens to them?"

The General Gnome shrugged. "We kill them, of course."

Snotty gave a careless nod.[36]

Snotty and the General rode away from the Bazaar and the end

---

36   Betrayal of friendship is a common motif in fairy and folk tales of all lands. Again, a fruitful area for study. Dr. Fallaize has shown that when such motifs are this common, there is a biological basis for them. (See Fallaize, year 61.) In studies in collaboration with the Hanuman School of Healing (formerly the Hanuman School of Medicine and Veterinary Study), Dr. Fallaize has shown that illnesses such as Betrayal of a Friend, Cruelty to Those Weaker Than Oneself, and Building Oneself Up at the Expense of Others, long thought to be moral illnesses alone, actually can be measured in physical symptoms. An excellent example of this in an Arcadian fairy tale is "Reine the Fox," where the vanity of the Princess shows itself in a persistent rash on her left thigh. (See Vale, year 26.)

of the Great Lawn, out onto the glowing desert, which stretched to the foothills and mountains beyond. As they rode, Snotty listened, all attention as the General discoursed on the Way of the Gnome.

The General pointed to the Peak that jutted up before them, dominating the landscape, the Peak that had impressed Snotty so much before. "Its name is the Peak of Transcendence," he said. "Every Gnome's desire. The white, the icy, the glorious Peak!" Seeing the Peak like that, chill and grand on the horizon, made Snotty feel hot and restless and bothered. A gust of yearning for even more grandeur than this rushed through him. "What's better than a Sun God?" he wondered. "King? Emperor? What?" His head throbbed and his limbs burned. His tongue was dry. His eyes hurt. His throat rasped. "I'll be it, whatever it is! Whatever it is, I'll do it!"

"The Peak!" he thought fervently. "That's it! I'll conquer the Peak!"

"Ah, General," Snotty said, forcing himself to speak casually. "Any of your bunch ever climbed the Peak before?"

"Never," the General said in a hushed voice. "He who would lead us to the Peak of Transcendence would be the Greatest Of Them All!"

Snotty nodded in what he hoped was a cool sort of way. Inside, though, he was seething. "Fine!" he thought in a fever of plans. "The Greatest Of Them All! That's for me! Right!" Snotty did not know it, but these were Gnomic ambitions he felt. Now that he was the Sun God, they had become his as well.

It was this Fever with which Snotty now burned. And it burned every thought of everything but the Peak of Transcendence out of his mind.

Chapter VIII

IN THE FORTRESS OF THE GNOMES

"We'll start," the General Gnome announced as they rode through the tall gray metal gates of the Fortress of the Gnomes, "with the Grand VIP Tour."

"Suits me," said Snotty. He was impressed by his surroundings, though of course he didn't show this. The Gnomes of the Fortress cheered his arrival, and the appetizing aroma of the Feast ahead filled the air.

The Fortress itself, a solid mass of concrete and flat gray trim, was a showcase of advanced technology and security. Everywhere, for example, were screens of the largest possible size. Each one showed what was going on somewhere else, whether in the Fortress, or on the Plains outside.

"Handy, those," the General grunted. He tried, and failed, to keep a note of pride from his voice. "We've got everything under control—everything boxed in! Not a leaf falls without us knowing it—not that there are many of those left, now that we're almost through fixing up the Garden." The General gave a genial chuckle. "No, Snotty, nothing gets by a Gnome! No Angel, no Fairy Tale creature—certainly no Rebel. Can't have any of them coming round here, now, can we?"

"I should say not," Snotty said gruffly. He didn't know what Rebels the General was talking about, and as for Angels or Fairy Tale Creatures—he didn't even want to think about it, really. And of course he knew better than to ask.

A waiting Gnome took the reins of his rocking horse, and Snotty and the General Gnome dismounted, continuing the Tour on foot.

An entourage of Gnomes followed at a respectful distance.

"As you see, Snotty, Gnome Technology is the finest in all the worlds," the General said. "It is second to none in its ability to put EACH AND EVERY THING IN ITS VERY OWN BOX!"

Snotty nodded. He could see the truth of this with his own eyes. Everywhere around him were boxes. Security boxes, dispatch boxes, telecommunications boxes, boxes of supplies—stacks and stacks of boxes of all kinds reached up to the top of the Fortress walls. All of this impressed him.

They paused at a smaller set of screens. On them, Gnomes rushed here and there. The Feast was being prepared.

"The Kitchen," the General said, pointing. "Anything you want them to make, you just let me know."

Snotty nodded his satisfaction.

"I see all my favorite foods, General," he said.

"Yes," the General said. "There's nothing like a real Feast." They watched as two Lambs turned a whole sheep on a spit. And Snotty's mouth watered as the Gnome Pastry Chef gave a last touch to a tall chocolate cake covered with chocolate whipped cream.

"Yum," Snotty said in spite of himself. He suspected this was not something a Sun God would say. Still, the General didn't seem to notice.

"Sir, where do you want this Monster, SIR?" bellowed a Gnome. The Dragon stood there, head bowed. The Gnome held it by a silver chain.

Snotty frowned. He didn't know what he wanted to do with the Dragon.

"Of course, Snotty expects you to tether the Monster in a secure place and await further instructions," the General barked.

Snotty nodded. "Might come in handy," he said, trying to look wise.

All the Gnomes beamed at this. "Snotty's right, as usual," the

General Gnome said. "This Monster will be useful in battle."

"That's what I was thinking," Snotty said, his expression lofty and serene. But to himself, he thought, "What battle? Where? With WHAT?"

Rifle fire sounded from the other side of the Fortress wall.

"Target practice, eh?" Snotty said.

"In a way," the General said, smiling as if Snotty had been very witty. "The firing squad. They're getting ready for tomorrow."

Snotty, startled, thought of Snowflake. He wiped a hand across his forehead. It and his cheeks were very hot. But then there was the Great Wall of the Fortress to admire, and the moment passed.

It was a cunning thing, the Great Wall. Woven of jagged metal, it encircled the fort.

"Can't get through that," the General Gnome said. "Impenetrable. Im-pen-e-tra-ble!"

"What's it made of?" Snotty took hold of a bit of the wall, which was formed of silver links so tiny that they appeared as a seamless whole. It was a dangerous looking thing, all right.

"Prejudices," the General Gnome said.

"What?" Snotty said.

"Stupid views," the General explained. "Strongly held opinions with little or no basis in fact." He and Snotty looked up in silence at the Great Wall, admiring the sheer genius of the Gnome invention. "Our architects asked themselves, what's the one thing that's impossible to breach? The answer was obvious! Nothing gets past a stupid prejudice."

"You're proud of Gnome technology, General."

"As proud as a Gnome can be." The General Gnome wiped a tear from his eye. "GT will be the saving of the Plains. Of course," he continued matter-of-factly, "no progress without struggle! As Mr. Big says, we must destroy the Plains in order to save them."

Snotty froze. Mr. Big? Was Mr. Big here? No. He couldn't be. It must be some other Mr. Big.

Agitated, Snotty only half-listened as the General pointed out the other sights. Gnome and boy made their way now through winding corridors. The General wanted to show Snotty to his quarters before the Grand Feast.

So rattled was Snotty that he hardly noticed the grandeur of his Gnome-sized rooms. There were his evening clothes, too, his first set ever, laid out on the satin coverlet of the enormous bed. But instead of savoring the moment, he just threw them on any old which way. He kept thinking: Who was Mr. Big? And what was he doing here?

In Megalopolis, Snotty claimed he worked for Mr. Big. "But of course it's a lie. There's no Mr. Big. I made him up," he thought.

At every moment, though, he felt less and less certain about the truth of this. "Because," he thought, "somehow I've always known that Mr. Big DOES exist, that I DIDN'T invent him." But how could Snotty know such a ridiculous thing: that Mr. Big both did and didn't exist? How could these two things be true at the same time?[37]

Had the Gnomes invented a Mr. Big of their own? Or was Mr. Big here—really here?

"And what does it mean if he IS?" Snotty wondered. He was still wondering when the General came to escort him to the Grand Feast.

The Grand Feast was, of course, in the Grand Hall. (Snotty quickly got used to the fact that, with the Gnomes, everything was Grand.) Hundreds of solemn Gnomes, in full military or evening dress, their decorations blazing in the light of the fluorescent chandeliers above, sat in rows at a series of dark gray metal tables covered with gray plastic

---

37   A question I plan to cover in my monograph *Lives of Things That Go Bump in the Night: A Meditation on Dreams and Their Dreamers.* It is, alas, too complex an issue to be dealt with conclusively here. I will say, however, that the larger question—how different, even opposing worlds can exist at the same time—is a basic question for Arcadian physics. I have long maintained that not only can this be so, but it is so, to the loud and public scorn of the followers of Professor Grayling and his Neofundamentalist school.

cloths and flat gray silver. They drank from pewter goblets. Sheep servants bustled around them, covering every surface with platters of steaming lamb roasted to a gray turn.

"Herrrrmmm... errrrrmmm... eerrrrrrm." There was a buzz of interest as Snotty entered, and then applause as the General escorted him to the place of honor. When Snotty sat, the entire room leapt to its feet. The General Gnome proposed a toast: "To Snotty!" he cried. And the Gnomes replied in manly chorus: "To Snotty! To Snotty! To Snotty!"

Snotty acknowledged this tribute with an urbane smile. "Er, General," he said as they began the meal. "Mr. Big. Will he be joining us?"

At this, the General roared with laughter, slapping his knee. He passed on what Snotty had said to the next Gnome, who passed it on to the next, and so on. Soon the entire Hall chuckled at this display of wit. And with that Snotty had to be satisfied. He didn't dare ask again.

This was the night of Snotty's triumph. He was toasted, and he toasted in return. It seemed to him that he had never been so witty or so sophisticated. He'd got the knack of holding one hand in his evening jacket pocket with the kind of rakish elegance he had seen on TV. There was much manly banter and he joined right in. "Just as if," he thought, "I was actually a Man!" He wished with all his heart that Mr. Big could see him now. If Mr. Big existed, of course.

At one point in the evening, Snotty noticed a woman in the room. There was only one. She had not taken part in the toasts, or in the foods of the Feast: at her place was a bit of bread and a cup of water. She got up to excuse herself, and, as she passed, each Gnome leapt up and touched his forehead with a gesture of respect. You could see why. She was modest, but there was something formidable about her, too.

"That's Justice," the General Gnome said. "She's on our side, as you see."

Snotty looked at her, fascinated. Justice was a tall woman, with everything about her practical and no nonsense, from her gray helmet of hair to her sensible shoes.

"Justice," he said. "I thought she was blind."

"She is," the General said. "Blind as a bat without her glasses." And Snotty noticed the black-rimmed glasses she wore on the end of her nose.[38]

He would have asked more, but just then the Bardic Gnome entered, sweeping a low bow to Justice as she, coolly nodding, went out. It was this Gnome's task to recite the after dinner poems recounting the Noble Deeds of the Gnomes. He wore a gold wreath around his head, and he declaimed his tale in a voice that filled the hall.

"Listen to my tale [the Bardic Gnome began] of the Gnomes of yore. How we came to these Plains and conquered them, for the good of all people, creatures, animals, vegetables and minerals thereon.

"Many, many years ago, our Ancestor Gnomes lived on the Great Lawn in the Sky. They formed the Great Circle, and one day, at the Great Council in the Great Circle, the Great Big Gnome spoke out. He said: 'This lawn is good. But good is not Great, and we Gnomes are Great. We must not keep our Greatness to ourselves! We must search out new lands to impress with our Greatitude. We must carry our message of Greatness to all! This is our DESTINY!'

"The Ancestor Gnomes agreed with the Great Big Gnome's sage words. So they prayed to Mr. Big. And Mr. Big, who answers the prayers of all who serve him (may he be praised a Great Many Times), granted their wish. A Great Hole opened up in the Great Lawn, and

---

38   A stylistic mistake by the unknown author. Naming characters allegorically is a low
form of literature, another observation for which I am indebted to Professor Grayling.
The teller of this tale is concerned less with literary quality than with expressiveness,
again a common trait of the folk and fairy tale.

the Ancestor Gnomes jumped down and down and down into the bowels of the Sky until they came to our Great World.

"This was the Dawn of Time."

Snotty looked around. Every Gnome was still, except for the moving lips of some, who silently recited along with him the words of the Bardic Gnome.

"Eons passed [the Bardic Gnome went on]. The Gnomes fought for their Great Destiny. You know, oh my Brothers, of the Greatness of Gnomic Deeds!"

"Hear hear!" cried a Gnome with an eye patch. There was a solemn pounding of pewter goblets on gray metal tables in response.

"Acre by acre we conquered the Plains. Closer and closer have we moved to our Great Goal."

At this, there was a collective intake of Gnome breath. Snotty looked on, eyes shining. The Great Goal! It would be his Great Goal as well!

"Our Great Goal, oh my Gnomic Brothers: to conquer the PEAK OF TRANSCENDENCE!"

"YES!" Snotty shouted, jumping up with his fist in the air.

The Bardic Gnome, flattered by this attention on the Sun God's part, gave a creaky bow and went on. He told of Great Battles with the creatures that fled from the Plains to the fastness of the Mountains of Resistance. "Those foul mountains that ring the Great Peak! They hide those base Rebels, those who hate our Freedoms and our Gnomic Destiny!"

"Let's GET 'EM!" Snotty yelled.

"Hear hear!" another Gnome shouted. "Hear hear!" the Gnomes shouted all around.

The Bardic Gnome told now of those Gnomes of yore who found the one secret way to the Peak undefended by the Rebels. "The Pretty Pass! That fatal snowy way! Remember, oh Gnomes, the many thousands of our people frozen alive as they came to the Pretty Pass.

Thousands of Gnomes bonded to its rocks forever in the frozen air!"

"That's bad," Snotty said and frowned.

"But the SUN GOD has been foretold!" the Bardic Gnome boomed. All eyes turned to Snotty, whose face glowed hot and red. "He it is who will THAW the Pretty Pass, gateway to the Peak of Transcendence, and enable us to conquer the Great Peak. This was promised by Gnomic Prophets since before the Dawn of Time!"

Snotty ducked his head. He felt very hot. Was it possible he was going to do all that? "Well, why not?" he thought. "I've done all right at everything else I've tried. Why not at being a Sun God, too?" So he sat straight up and raised another defiant fist in the air.

The Great Hall erupted. The Gnomes were on their feet now, tears in their eyes, stomping and yelling, cheering the Sun God who would lead them to Victory.

It was the Apotheosis of Snotty. The high point of his life. "This," he thought earnestly to himself as he acknowledged the accolades of the masses, "is what I was born for."

He took bow after bow until his head spun.

"If only," he thought, coming up for air, "If only I could feel it. I mean, that I am the Sun God." He took a drink from his goblet and felt he almost had the Greatness of it in his grasp. He hadn't thought about Snowflake all night, not once, not at all. He had made his way to the top. Nothing could stop him now.

The Gnomes cheered and cheered. "Hooray! Hooray for Snotty! Hooray for Snotty the Sun God!"

His body burned with desire for the Peak and with the Fever of the Plains.

But the funny thing was, except for that, he couldn't feel a thing.

Chapter IX

MEANWHILE, IN THE MOUNTAINS

Outside on the Plains, a full moon shone. There wasn't a cloud in the sky. You could see every stunted tree, every bare boulder, every bit of nasty scrub grass as clear as if it were day. And besides, no one would dare to assault such an impenetrable fortress. So the Guard Gnomes, watching from their towers jutting up from the Wall, found their job an easy one.

It was true what the General Gnome said about Gnome Technology. Not the smallest infraction against Gnome Greatness escaped it. Nothing outside of that Greatness had a chance.

It was troubling that there was still an Enemy, but there wasn't a Gnome among them who didn't believe it was a matter of time before that Enemy too was history. The Gnomes didn't worry much about the Rebels: a ragtag muddle of dreamers and toys and animals and gardeners, not a trained fighter in the whole pathetic bunch. Rank amateurs who fought only when they had to—"if you can imagine anything so unprofessional!" as the General Gnome said to Snotty with the after dinner port.

No, the Gnomes had nothing but contempt for the Rebels, who never crept out of their mountain home. "Country bumpkins!" snorted the General Gnome. "They'd rather grow flowers and drink chocolate than fight like men!" There had been much laughter at this. Snotty joined in.

Snotty did wonder how, if what the General said was true, the Rebels could be an actual threat. But he didn't like to ask.

"Why don't we just head up the mountains and get 'em?" he said instead, and the General looked at him with that approval that warms the heart of the Sun God wherever he may reign.

"Well, we would, you know," the General confided, and poured Snotty another bumper of port. "Only we can't figure out the paths that go around the Pretty Pass. We can't figure them out at all. Look...." Here he spilled some salt onto the gray table top and traced out a rough map with his knife. "There's some kind of path like a goat track, back and forth, back and forth through the scrub. We've never found it. And spies have told us there is a wider road, made of white stone"—Snotty frowned as a vague memory tugged at him—"but the thing must be hiding in plain sight, because we can't find that one either, no matter how hard we try! Not on our own, anyway." Here he gave Snotty a penetrating look. "We look to you, Snotty! You have been foretold. It's you who will show us the way up the Path of Care. It's you who will brave the Path of Solitude!"

Snotty had a gratifying vision of himself dressed in shining armor, leading a charge up the mountains toward the Peak of Transcendence, trampling what was left of the Rebels—or spearing, or shooting, or bombing them ("whatever," he thought in his enthusiasm)—in his eagerness to get to the top.

He gave a happy little burp, and all around him the manly Gnomes beamed.

Meanwhile, above the Plains, over the Mountains, a Star shone in the East.[39] Not one of the Guard Gnomes bothered to look up—their

---

39   The motif of Star as Angel, and Angel as Star, appears in Arcadian folk and fairy tales with endearing frequency. This tale is no exception. Only one recorded case of an actual angel has ever been known in Arcadia, the Angel invited by Sophia the Wise to become a Minister of Arcadian State. Yet the motif is common. See, for instance, "The Queen of the Sky," in which a passing Angel is mistaken for a queen by a woodcutter;

job was to guard the Plains, not the sky—so not one of them saw the Star (if that, indeed, was what it was) move across the sky, in a way very strange for a Star. Stranger still, this one made a rustling noise as it went, as if from the flapping of wings. Stars don't have wings, of course. But this one certainly did. And no matter what it was, it shone with the brightest light of anything in the sky, brighter, even, than the Moon Itself. As it approached the Gnome Fortress, its light streamed down onto the gray towers.

Falling under this light, the Gnomes on the battlements below stretched out their arms and smiled. Each Gnome yawned, and nodded, and then, still smiling, fell asleep. Every so often one would give a forlorn yelp, as if dreaming of somewhere far away, where Gnomes sat in a circle on a Great Lawn telling stories and smoking cigars.

While the Guard Gnomes slept, a black bank of clouds swept over the sky, covering the moon.

Reversals like this, fast and unexpected, happen in the desert.

Everywhere was black. The sky was an impenetrable velvet cloth. The Guard Gnomes snored on. There was not a movement to be seen on the Plains. Except... what was that at the very edge of the foothills of the Mountains, right where they meet the Plains, on the banks of the Stream where it runs into the River there? Was that a prick of light? Did it flash and then go out?

Or was it nothing after all?

Probably nothing.

The Guard Gnomes slept on.

The wind blew the clouds fast across the moon and tore the velvet

---

"The Three Wishes," where a woodcutter's daughter makes three wishes on three stars and has them granted by three angels; and "The Tale of a Blue Star," told by an angel to a group of Arcadian woodcutters' children. In Megalopolis, there are no tales of angels, with the exception of the folk tale "Why the Angels Left." Curiously, there is a similar motif at the start of *Snotty Saves the Day*. (See Vale, year 22; Vale, year 26.)

curtain in one long jagged tear. In that half light, a Gnome might have spotted a single line of moving figures, muffled and hooded and masked, heading across the open Plains toward the Fortress. But when the wind mended the tear in the clouds and the Plains turned black again, he wouldn't have been able to say if that single file of movement had been real or just a trick of the desert light.

The dangers of approaching the Fortress of the Gnomes were legendary. No one would take the risk of crossing the open desert out of cover of the Mountains. No one would be fool enough to try. No one ever had tried. Every Gnome knew that.

But these were desperate days for the enemies of the Gnomes. And there were strange stirrings in the Mountains of Resistance.

Chapter X

KIDNAPPED!

After the Grand Feast, Snotty retired to his rooms accompanied by his Entourage.

This Entourage was made up of the highest-ranking Gnomes. You could tell this because of the noise from the many decorations clanking on their gnomish chests. These medals made so much noise as the group made its progress through the halls that Snotty couldn't understand a word of the conversation that went on over his head.

"Mmmmmmmmr... mrrrr... and so we see that errr... the grand assault pprrr... of course, we Gnomes have always aaawwwrrr...." That was what it sounded like. Every so often, the sound of the rrrsssss meant the speaker had made a joke. Then the other Gnomes laughed.

Snotty inclined his head in what he hoped was a stately way and did what everyone else did. In this way he acted wisely, as many a Great Leader has before.

At one point, the murmuring ended clearly in a question. It sounded something like this: "And so... gggrrr... your position... ssssrrrrrrr?"

Everyone looked at Snotty.

Snotty cocked his head. One finger touched his cheek. Then he said, "Vvvrrrrrr...ooooppppphhhrrrrr....grraaaannndddeeeuurrrrr!"

He nodded curtly to show that he was finished.

The Entourage stopped its progress to listen with greater care. All of the August Dignitaries were much struck by the wisdom—more than the wisdom, the plain good sense—of their Sun God. Nodding with respectful enthusiasm, they burst into a spontaneous round of applause. And with many exchanges of incomprehensible compliments ("lllrrrrr... nnrrrrr... mmmmmssssttt... hhnnnrrrrddddd...") they bowed him into his suite.[40]

"Bye-bye! Thanks for the great evening, guys! See you tomorrow! Sleep tight!" Snotty bowed and bowed until the door shut and he was alone. Then he turned and surveyed his Grand Suite.

"Wow," he said.

It was really grand. There was gray carpet so thick that Snotty's feet sank into it up to his ankles. There was pale gray linen on the enormous, Gnome-sized, gray metal bed. Laid on the silver satin coverlet were pajamas embroidered on the breast pocket with a silver Sun. There was a gray wood writing desk with a gray-shaded lamp, set before a huge gray leather chair. And the bath! That was gray and white marble with platinum spigots in the shape of birds. The towels beside it were so large and soft that Snotty could have curled up and slept in one.

"No one in Megalopolis—even the best parts—has a room like this," Snotty thought with satisfaction.

Now Snotty believed in his star. For twelve years he had known he was destined for greatness. "And I was right!" he said, bouncing up and down on the bed. "Keep going and things can only get bigger, better, grander, more important still! Snotty the KING! Snotty the EMPEROR! Snotty the SUN GOD! HAH!"

But to tell the truth, Snotty was not enjoying himself as much as he could have been. He was feverish—hot and restless—and he couldn't stand still.

"It's stuffy in here," he muttered uneasily, loosening the collar of his evening shirt. "And I'm not used to all that rich food." He bounced up and down a couple more times, but it wasn't all that

---

40 I confess I am compelled to give in to a most unscholarly impulse here, and say that, in my days of Government and University administration, I chaired many a meeting very like this one of Snotty's!

much fun after all. "Maybe I need some fresh air."

The doors that led to the balcony were Gnome-sized, of course, and the door handle was above his head, but he solved this by pushing and pulling at the gray leather steps that were meant to help him into the Gnome-sized bed. Once he had those in place, it was easy to climb up, push down on the handle and go out the door. A moment's work and Snotty was on the Gnome-sized balcony, breathing the night air of the Plains.

There were no stars. The sky was black. The wind whistling across the Plains made him shiver and cling to a balcony pillar. This was also Gnome-sized, and Snotty had to take care to keep an arm wrapped around its massive post, otherwise he might have fallen through the man-sized space in between.

From up there, Snotty had a wonderful view of the Wall of Prejudice. Its closely woven material glittered in the guard tower lights. Snotty enjoyed the sight of it rippling in the desert wind.

As he admired it, he saw—just out of the corner of his eye— something wrong. "No," he thought, shaking his head. "Can't be something there. Everything's the way it always is. Must be seeing things." Still, when he looked closer, he saw a shadow... a glimmer... nothing definite. "No. Yes. Wait. There it is again!" It was impossible. But there it was.

Something pushed at the fabric of the Wall of Prejudice. An unknown force punched a hole through it, piercing it from the outside. "What is it?" Snotty thought, excited. So excited was he by the novelty of the situation that he forgot the danger.

A hole worked its way open in the shimmering links of the Wall. By degrees it grew bigger and bigger until it was as big as Snotty himself. And then through it, breaching the Wall of Prejudice, came a dozen weird beings.

Snotty had never seen anything like them before.

Each one was compact, cylinder shaped, multi-colored, and

springy—like a short, squat pogo stick. These bounced up and down on the ground. Snotty could hear them. "Boing... boing... boing..."

What were they?

What could possibly breach the Wall of Prejudice?

Snotty didn't recognize them. How could he? These were Ideas. Snotty hadn't come across many Ideas in Megalopolis, and certainly no brand new ones, shiny and bright, like these. They looked amusing, even laughable, and small. It's an odd fact that Ideas like this frequently turn out to be the most formidable of all.[41] But of course Snotty didn't know this, and he didn't realize their power until seven small figures, hooded and masked, appeared through the breach in the Wall made by them.

Too late Snotty realized the danger. "GENERAL!" he shouted. "The ENEMY! Sound the ALARM!"

At this, a hooded intruder looked up, eyes glittering through the slits in its mask. Calmly, it plucked an Idea off the ground and hurled it straight at Snotty.

He ducked just in time. The Idea flew over his shoulder and landed on a Guard as he sounded the klaxon horn. But the Idea just bounced off and landed on the railing of the tower where it teetered this way and that.

The raiders disappeared, then reappeared weighed down by a large bundle. As they hurried toward the hole, from this bundle fell a pair of black reading glasses.

"They've got Justice!" Snotty yelled. He heard sounds from the far side of the Fortress: neighings, snortings, squealings, shoutings. From this, Snotty knew the Rebels had set the caged Monsters free.

"Snowflake?" Snotty thought. He had a second's doubt before

---

41 Again, see Law of the Small (Bender Boyce-Flood, year 17). The Law states that in any cultural dead end, it is from the smallest, most outcast, most scorned section of the culture that future hope comes. And it is this law that is the ideological battleground of our present civil war.

pushing it away and shouting: "To arms! To arms! Gnomes, to arms!"

The Gnomes answered the call of their Sun God, running from all directions and waving huge weapons. They had no chance to use these, however. The Rebels engaged them in hand-to-hand combat, and in this the weapons were of no use. The Gnomes were trained to attack and kill the Enemy at a distance, not, as it were, man to man. So even though these raiders were no higher than three feet tall, and even though there were only seven of them, and even though Justice weighed them down, their desperate bravery and unexpected tactics won their escape. Many a Gnome fell, hacked at the knee, or punctured in the bunion. In a flash the Rebels were through the hole in the Wall of Prejudice, back out on the Plains, free—and with Justice, too.

"No!" Snotty wailed. The Guard Gnome above swung his klieg light to the outside of the Fortress wall and nicked the Idea teetering there on the railing's edge. The Idea tumbled off and down and hit Snotty a good smack right on the back of the head.

"OW!" yelped Snotty, clapping his hand over it and yanking with all his might. But the Idea stuck to Snotty no matter what he did. He yowled and pulled with his other hand, trying to get rid of it the way you try to get rid of a wasp whose stinger is already too far in. In his frantic attempt to get away from the Idea, Snotty lost his balance and tumbled off the edge of the balcony, falling to the ground below.

Snotty watched the courtyard hurtle up toward him. He shut his eyes and waited for the end. But this time there wasn't one. Instead the Idea, sticking to Snotty, pulled him back up. Snotty was amazed at the strength of it. For a minute there, he almost enjoyed himself, swooping low over the ground, pulled along by the Idea. He would have enjoyed himself, anyway, if it hadn't made for the breach in the Wall of Prejudice and headed for the desert outside.

Chapter XI
DAWN IN THE MOUNTAINS OF RESISTANCE

"NNOOO!!!" Snotty wailed. Lightning flashed. Thunder cracked. The Fortress lights disappeared behind him in the dark. Another crack of thunder and the sky opened up. Sheets of rain poured down—sluices of water—as often happens in a desert storm. These are sudden and fierce, and this one stopped the Gnomes from giving chase.

So the Rebels disappeared into the darkness. And Snotty went with them. Well, he had no other choice.

Snotty's Idea dragged him skittering across the desert floor. Snotty squealed as he bounced off a rock, and just when he thought he couldn't be any more uncomfortable, the Idea veered out of the rain up an old mountain track. This path was covered with so many bramble bushes and nettle patches that Snotty became seriously annoyed.

But Snotty had never been one to see the glass as half empty. "At least the rain stopped," he said cheerfully to himself as his Idea slowed down. Snotty, wincing as his bare feet made one last awkward bounce against a tree stump (he'd long since lost the gentlemen's brocade slippers given him by the Gnomes), saw they'd come onto a clearing, a sheltered meadow, on the mountainside. This was misty in the pale pre-dawn. Nothing was clear. Muffled and stocky figures moved in and out of the fog. Snotty could just make out their low murmurs as he and his Idea passed by.

Who were these figures? Were they dangerous? What were they doing there? And what would they do to him, Snotty?

The morning cold was sharp and harsh, and Snotty, let down on the meadow grass by his Idea, felt frost crackle between his toes. His teeth chattered.

"Here." A small figure loomed up at him from out of the thickening mist. It thrust something hot and steaming at him, and disappeared again.

Cautiously, Snotty eyed the warm thing in his hands. It looked delicious—pale brown and creamy and sprinkled with spices on top. And it smelled wonderful. He sniffed at it and frowned.

It was hot chocolate, of course. But Snotty had never tasted this before. He wasn't sure about it now.

"Hey," a high-pitched, girlish voice said, and another, even smaller, figure, appeared, eyes glittering behind its mask. Snotty recognized this as the Rebel who had thrown the Idea at him.

"That can't be right," he thought, offended that he'd been bested by a girl. And then, grudgingly, "She seems friendly enough."

"Drink up," she said encouragingly. "Don't let it get cold." Two other masked Rebels appeared beside her, holding their own mugs, which they raised in a friendly salute before laughing and disappearing together into the now thick fog.

"Were they laughing at me?" Snotty wondered as he sipped at the hot drink, first doubtfully, then with more and more enthusiasm. It hadn't sounded like it, but you could never be sure. Snotty hated being laughed at. In fact, of the five things he most hated—being laughed at, being hungry, being helpless, being ignored, being looked down on—it was in the top three. So he was anxious not to run into those girls again until he was sure of their intent. He picked his way slowly through the fog.

Careful as he was, though, he almost stumbled over two tall women giving each other a hug. "Sorry," he mumbled. He turned away. But the two women looked as if they knew all about him, and one of them put out a hand to hold him back.

"So you got here, did you?" she said, and Snotty then recognized her face.

"Justice!"

Justice looked at him as if she wasn't too pleased with what she saw, and let him go. The other woman smiled and held out a slim brown hand. "Ah," she said. "You must be the Sun God." She looked like Justice, but her hair was wilder and streaked with gray. "My name is Mercy," she said.

"The Sun God," Justice snorted as Snotty and Mercy shook hands. "Indeed."

"Pleased to meet you," Mercy said.

"No need to be so formal," Justice said briskly. "I had a good look at him at the Feast. He's just a snotty little boy."

This stung.

"I AM the Sun God," Snotty said, stamping his foot. "I'm Snotty the Sun God!" Confused and angry, he turned back into the fog. The words "just a snotty little boy" rang unpleasantly in his ears.

He walked on, brooding on this and clutching an empty mug, up a green rise. He was aggrieved that Justice and Mercy hadn't recognized his greatness. But then, in all fairness—because Snotty was a very fair boy—he had to admit that he didn't look like much this morning. "Not that I do even on my best days!" he thought, and he laughed. The fog lightened now and the newly risen sun burned what was left of it away. Snotty could see farther, to the top of the hill, where there was a large white tent. In front of this, an enormous figure waved a stocky arm.

"Aha!" Snotty thought. "The Leader!"

Suddenly, he saw he wasn't as alone as he had thought. Dozens and dozens of muffled figures streamed around him up the hill. They didn't take much notice of him except to give a friendly nod now and then as they passed. As the Sun moved higher, the figures shed their hats and their mufflers and their coats, and Snotty saw that they were, most of them, Teddy Bears. Scattered among these Bears was the occasional Doll or low flying Kite. Snotty also thought he saw a large Gingerbread Man in lavender boots. But most of the others were Teddies, of all different colors and types of fur. The burly figure, the Leader, was much bigger than the others, a black and yellow Big Teddy with black button eyes.

This Big Teddy waddled down the hill toward Snotty, huge stubby paw outstretched, black button eyes unblinking. "Welcome," it said in a deep warm voice, and Snotty, exasperated, heard that this Bear, too, was a she. "Hello. Happy to see you. Glad you could come."

"YOU'RE the Enemy?" Snotty demanded, ignoring the outstretched paw. He gave an angry laugh. He thought of how scared and uncomfortable he had been, and this made him even madder.

The black and yellow Teddy stopped, dismayed. "Oh, the Enemy, well, I don't know about that," she said. After a moment, embarrassed, she dropped her paw.

She waved at the Bears behind and around her, and, as the fog had now entirely burned away, Snotty could see hundreds of them, standing silent in all directions. They peered at him anxiously.

This just exasperated him. Was this the Grand War of the Gnomes? This?

"We're not much for a fight," Big Teddy said finally, shuffling her huge black and yellow plush feet. "Unless we have to be, of course." A Bear or two behind her shook their heads in agreement. "But," she said, her round face brightening, "we're great ones for a picnic. And we love company. We always have. Known for it, in fact. So if you would just..."

"A PICNIC!" Snotty scowled with contempt.

Big Teddy fell backward with a thud, onto her plush rear, as if Snotty's voice had knocked her down. Other Teddies rushed to her side. But she waved them away and, huffing, pulled herself up as well as she could. "They're nice, our picnics," she said in a mild way.

"This is unbelievable," Snotty snorted. "I come here, expecting

Rebel Forces, Guerrilla Warriors, getting ready to make war on the Grand Army of the Gnomes..."

"Oh," Big Teddy sighed. "Yes. Well. We're that, too, you know."

Snotty stared. "Oh, yeah," he jeered. "You're the guys who're going to beat the Gnomes. Teddy Bears! TEDDY BEARS! A bunch of stupid, crummy, little Teddy B..."

But he never had a chance to finish the sentence. Big Teddy sighed, the Teddy Bears sighed, and with a sad nod, she strode forward with one...two...three strides of her enormous black and yellow stubby legs and, with one blow from her enormous plush paw, knocked Snotty a powerful clout on the head.

The hit, when it came, was like velvet, like the roaring of a faraway lion, like being tumbled in a warm sea. Snotty, outraged, had time to think indignantly: "This doesn't hurt at all!" Then he toppled to the ground.

And all of his nasty, niggling little thoughts were, for the moment anyway, at an end.

Chapter XII

SNOTTY FINDS THE KEY

A voice cleared itself in a polite sort of way.
"Er...mmmrreeehhmmp," it said. "Ermp."

Snotty's nose twitched. He woke up. He couldn't remember where he was. He opened his eyes. The face of a silly-looking teddy bear hung upside down above him.

"HEY!" he shouted in surprise. He shut his eyes tight. Maybe when he opened them, the thing would have gone away.

"Oh dear, oh dear, oh dear," muttered a silly-sounding voice. "Oh dear, oh dear...." Snotty heard little stumpy plush footsteps move away across a wooden floor.

When they retreated, he opened his eyes again. There was nothing there—nothing but a ceiling of woven tree boughs. These were of spruce and cedar, and they smelled good.

"Ermp... erm... ERM." The voice cleared its throat. Snotty sat up and looked around. There, almost invisible against the brown and cream woven boughs of the wall, was the silly-looking and sounding Bear. He was brown and cream colored, too.

"Pardon," the Bear said. "Didn't mean to startle you."

Snotty blinked.

The Bear was indeed a silly-looking thing. He was covered in brown and cream plush, and a pink felt tongue stuck out of his mouth. A baseball cap was sewn off balance over his bugged-out eyes.

In his paw, the Bear held a long, thin, rosy thing that he waved in the air.

"Thermometer," he said in a silly-sounding growl. "Nothing to be scared of. See?"

Snotty was about to dispute the idea that he would be scared of anything at all, let alone of such a thing, when the Bear waddled forward with a concerned expression on his silly face. (He had a limp in his left rear leg, which was a strange thing for a stuffed bear, Snotty thought.) The Bear held out the thermometer so that Snotty could see what it said. Written on its side in bold red letters was: "VERY ILL."

"No, I'm not!" Snotty protested. "Never felt better in my life!"

This was a lie, of course. Snotty's head throbbed in a horrible way, and his stomach twisted this way and that. In fact, everything hurt, even his toes and the tips of his fingers. "But I'm not telling a silly-looking bear that!" Snotty knew it was dangerous to be weak, unless you were among friends. And since he had never in his life been among friends, it would have been silly of him to change his behavior now.

The silly-looking Bear cocked his head.

"Definitely a case of fever," the Bear squeaked, nodding its silly plush head. "What we call Trance Fever, here in the Mountains. And very painful it is, too." Before Snotty could protest, the Bear laid the thermometer against his head.

"HEY!" Snotty yelled, batting it away. But not before he saw a new set of red letters form. These said: "BETRAYED HIS FRIEND."

"Oh DEAR," the silly-looking Bear said, his voice filled with real distress. "Oh my poor friend. Oh I'm so sorry."

"I didn't!" Snotty shouted, struggling to get up. But he felt groggy and achy and not himself, and it was like moving through Jell-O. "I DIDN'T, I tell you!" But the silly-looking Bear just stood there shaking his head, looking at Snotty with an unbearable—as it were—expression of sympathy on his silly face.

"How terrible," the Bear murmured. "How truly horrible and bad."

"I'm telling you," Snotty said, but his voice sounded weak and sneaky, even to him, "I didn't...."

"Sssh," said the Bear. He rummaged in a little black bag. "Let me give you something for the pain."

And he pulled from the bag a rose gold Key.

"No!" Snotty shouted as the Bear dipped the Key into a glass of water. "Don't touch me with that thing!" The sight of the Key filled him with dread, and he struggled to get away from it and from the Bear's horrible sympathy.

But his limbs ached, and he couldn't move. Exhausted and defeated, he fell back and closed his eyes. He felt the Bear place the Key gently right between his eyes. It felt cool and straight, and a softness, like a white light, spilled from it into Snotty's head. He felt this light spread through him, chasing away all the aches and pains it found, and as the last ache fled, Snotty drifted into sleep again, the same kind of sleep he'd fallen into when buffeted by Big Teddy's paw. But this time it was a slower fall, as if he were in a boat floating down a river on a summer's day. There was a pleasant rushing in his ears like the sound of water running over stones.

"Poor child," was the last thing he heard. "Poor, poor child." Then Snotty, for a time, heard nothing more.

———————

When he woke again, he felt much better. In fact, he felt excellent in every way. His headache and stomachache were gone. Nothing hurt in his limbs and his chest—nothing at all, except the throbbing where his little finger used to be. He was dressed now, not in his Gnome clothes, but in a lilac plush suit with matching boots. And he was hungry. He was very, very hungry.

"Feed me!" a voice said.

"Who said that?" Snotty leapt up, looking wildly around.

"Feed me!" the voice said again, very nearby—very. It took Snotty a moment to realize that it was the voice of his own stomach. Naturally, this was a bit of surprise.

"I didn't know you could talk," Snotty said to his stomach warily. He felt stupid talking to his own body parts like this, but he didn't know what else to do.

"I'm hungry," his stomach said, patient but insistent. Snotty wrinkled up his forehead and thought about this.

Snotty was used to being hungry. At such times, he knew, his stomach would complain until he stuffed down as much food as it could hold as fast as possible. (This was what he had done, for example, at the Gnomes' Grand Feast. Snotty felt sick afterwards, but he identified this feeling with pleasure as the sign of a true Feast.) "Ahem," his stomach said politely.

"Sorry," Snotty said. Looking around, he saw a woven twig and bark table, and on it were some slices of brown bread, a mound of milky cheese, and a bunch of scraped carrots.[42] Snotty looked at these doubtfully. He felt his stomach wasn't used to this kind of thing. He didn't know if it understood what it was in for.

"Now, please," his stomach said in a good-humored way.

"I don't know if you're going to like this," Snotty warned, trying an experimental chomp on a carrot. "And what if they're trying to poison us, huh?" But by now his stomach was too busy to reply.

The idea that the food might be poisoned cheered Snotty up a lot. It was making him nervous, all this Teddy Bear hospitality. It was not what he was used to. Whereas the thought that he was a prisoner, liable to be tortured or killed at any moment—if that was the position,

---

42   As previously remarked, food, and descriptions of food, are the hallmark of a classic Arcadian tale. This one is no exception. (See Vale, year 26, for other famous examples: "The Baker's Stone," and its tale of the miraculous sourdough bread, as well as the lavish meal the lovers share at the end of "Reine the Fox." Also see the famous Brunch with Death in the Maude Cycle.)

he knew where he was.

"More, please," his stomach said.

"Well," Snotty shrugged. "It's your funeral." So he ate his way through another couple of carrots and two slices of bread spread with the lemony cheese.

"Mmmm," his stomach said. But Snotty wasn't listening. Instead he planned his escape. Then he saw that the silly-looking Bear had left the rosy Key. There it was in the lock of the door.

"Honestly, what kind of a prison is this, anyway?" Snotty grumbled as he pocketed the Key in his lilac and purple plush suit. He slipped out the door. No one was about.

Snotty felt a little hurt by this. "What, they don't think I'm important enough to be guarded better than THIS?" Reflecting on the Bears' total lack of professionalism, he crossed a lush and overgrown meadow toward a wood where swallows and finches and chickadees sang in the trees. "I miss the Gnomes," he thought to himself, depressed. He missed their size and their strength. He missed their manliness and grandeur. Most of all, he missed his own importance in their midst. "But think of how much credit I'll get for escaping from the Rebel Stronghold with a full report. That'll be a real score!"

At the thought of this, Snotty cheered up. If it was war between the Gnomes and the Teddy Bears—as it obviously was—then he considered the Gnomes to be in the right. For one thing, they were bigger than the Bears.

That much was easy. Once Snotty had determined this, his duty was plain. "I must fight the Enemy by any means possible!" he thought fiercely. "First I should get the lay of the land." With that, he set about his mission with no delay. He went into the wood and climbed the highest tree.

As he climbed, the Key in his pocket slapped at his leg in an uncomfortable way. The higher Snotty got, the heavier the Key dragged on him.

Snotty ignored this.

When he had climbed as high as he could, he found himself in a canopy of treetops, surrounded on all sides by green: leaves, tree needles, and pale slanting light. He couldn't see up, he couldn't see down, he couldn't see around. And because the branches above him were spindly, this was as far as he could go.

Little pools of water dotted the canopy, places where rain collected in hollows made of twigs and leaves and lichen. Tiny transparent shrimp scuttled about. And in a pond cradled by a bowl of moss lay a rose pink Crab.

Snotty considered this. "A Crab in a tree," he thought. "That's weird." Other stuff was weird, too. The breeze smelled of strawberries. Every leaf and needle on every tree was clear and sharp. And, weirdest of all, the stump of Snotty's little finger stopped throbbing. Here, in the trees, it didn't hurt at all.

Snotty peered into the little pond. The rose pink Crab lay on its bottom, resting on a bed of pale green. Snotty leaned over to get a closer look, and the Key in his pocket banged against his leg.

"Let me out!" the Key said in a furious voice. "Now!"

Startled, Snotty thrust his hand in his pocket and pulled out the Key. It was heavier than he remembered, though, and it slipped from his hold and fell with a mild plop into the pool.

Snotty stared at the Key as it lay there at the bottom of the pond. Its head was oval and its shaft was plain. It was smooth and pink gold and it reminded Snotty of something, but he couldn't think of what. He dipped his hand in the water to get it back. To his surprise, the little pink Crab didn't scuttle away. Instead, to Snotty's even greater surprise, it put what might have been its shoulder—if crabs had shoulders—to the Key, as if trying to dislodge it from the moss.

Snotty was so surprised by this that he didn't do what he would have usually done—which would have been to pluck the Crab from the water, hold it by one pincer while it waved with the other, and then toss it to the forest floor below. Instead he was careful to touch the Key without touching the Crab.

He wondered why this was. As he grasped the Key, he had a strange thought. He thought he could feel what the Crab was feeling. Then it was more than a thought: it was real. He could feel it. He could feel cool water flow over his sturdy head, and he could see the wavy shimmer of the rose gold Key as the water moved. He could even see his own face—his, Snotty's face!—all waves and shimmers, peering from the surface above.

Startled again, Snotty pulled his hand away, leaving the Key behind.

A bird flew by, looking at him without much interest as it passed. It was yellow and black with a red splash on its head, and Snotty could see it flash from branch to branch.

Snotty shrugged and put his hand back in the pool, picking up the Key.

Then, all at once, he felt he was the Bird.

"Wow! That's terrific!" Snotty could feel the cross breezes that were too tiny for him to notice when he was only himself. He could feel how pleasantly those breezes ruffled the feathers on his breast. He could feel his smug pleasure in the beauty of his own song. And he could feel a tiny pang of bird hunger, and then feel patience, as he waited, singing, for a bug to pass by.

Snotty, enjoying himself as the bird, grabbed again at the Key and pulled it from the pond.

That was when it happened. As he held the Key tight, the world sprang up around him. Everywhere, in every corner, the world pulsed and buzzed and flowed. He could hear it. He could feel it. What was more, he knew it had always been there, only before he hadn't known.

"I can see it!" he said in his excitement. "I can see it now!" And it seemed to him that when he laughed at the sights, the sounds, the smells, the feelings around him—all connected together by the thinnest of webs—that the Crab and the Bird laughed with him. Everyone and everything connected to him by this web—and this was everyone and everything everywhere—laughed. Everywhere laughed One Great Laugh.

Snotty laughed so hard that his hand jerked out of the pond, yanking the Key from the water. It flew from his fingers and disappeared into the pale and dark green canopy of leaves. As it went, so did the web. The scene fell back to the quiet blank it had been before.

Snotty cried out and ran after the Key. He should have known better, of course; he had fallen like this before. But he didn't know better yet, so when he put his foot down too hard on a thin spot on the canopy, it happened again.

"Here I am, falling again," he said to himself in a detached way. And he did fall, even as he thought it, with a plop, into a cold clear stream. He didn't fight the current, and the stream carried him along. He found that when he ducked his head under its surface and opened his eyes, he could see a lot of things: tiny violet waving plants, and brightly colored fish—red and blue and yellow and white.

"Wait a minute," he thought. "I can't swim." But it seemed that he knew how, he had just forgotten. And so Snotty did a neat breaststroke into a pool that collected in swirls under some boulders at the side of the stream.

Snotty lay face up in that pool for a while, floating and looking at the clear blue evening sky as it deepened into twilight. In a corner was the rising crescent moon. A brilliant planet shone below it. A rosy light spread around the edges of the sky.

Toenails clicked on some boulders overhead. Snotty raised his eye and saw the Dog standing on a pink granite rock. Snotty scrambled out of the water to join him.

"Hello," he said. "You're here, too, are you?"

The Dog nodded and the two watched the sky as the sun made its final dip below the horizon, and stars burst out on its far side. Then the Dog shook his head, and Snotty knew what he meant as if he had said it out loud. "I never get tired of seeing that same sight in the sky."

"I know what you mean," Snotty agreed.

The Dog turned, his toenails clicking on the granite boulder, and headed back toward the meadow of the Teddy Bear camp. Snotty followed.

On the way, they passed Justice and Mercy sitting in the evening breeze, fanning themselves and talking. The women waved and nodded in a friendly way.

Up ahead in the meadow, two long rows of rough trestle tables stood, all laid with rush mats and wooden cups and bowls. There were platters of steaming greens and loaves of that same dark, sweet-smelling bread Snotty had eaten before. The talk of those sitting and helping themselves to the food rose and fell in a gentle stream.

As Snotty neared, though, silence fell. He stopped in confusion, and looked out over the still crowd, which stared back, it seemed to him, with mistrust and doubt. This stung, though he had to admit the justice of it—hadn't he laughed at them, called them nothing but stupid Bears?—and he turned to go. But there was a murmur from the crowd—"No, no!" a Crimson Bear protested, jumping up—and a general hubbub rose up. A Lemon Yellow Bear cleared a place on one of benches, and an Orange Bear leapt forward to lead Snotty to it and show him how to help himself to the food. He took some sweet smelling steamed nettles, pouring over them soup from a steaming tureen. A hunk of the bread and more of the lemony cheese completed his meal. The Crimson Bear pointed to a dish on which gray and white crystals were heaped. "There's the salt!" she said proudly, and Snotty recognized her as the masked Rebel who had braved the Gnome stronghold. She had looked much more frightening behind her mask. Now she just looked friendly and shy.

Snotty felt shy, too, but a Rose Pink Bear sprinkled some salt on his food and said, "It tastes better with it than without, don't you think?" Soon he was laughing and chatting with the Bears as if he had known them his whole life.

He had never laughed and chatted with anyone before as if he'd known them his whole life. In fact, the friends he had known his whole life were not the sort you would ever want to laugh and chat with—you had to be too careful to make sure you never let them get behind your back. You had to always keep an eye on them, and that, of course, got in the way of any real conversation.

Snotty knew he didn't have to worry about that here, with the Bears. So he just ate up and enjoyed himself in general.

During the meal, he looked around himself. There were many different kinds of Bears: stiff white ones with pink bows, black floppy ones with tartan jackets, skinny yellow ones, and a fat one that looked like it had been dragged by a cat.

And of course, he saw other creatures as well. There was a Lace Swan, and there was a Tin Soldier and a Rose Fairy, and there was the kind of Seaweed that goes pop when you sit on it. There was a Centaur and a group of Nymphs. There was a Pack of Playing Cards and a Leprechaun. There were at least seven Plastic Dinosaurs. And sitting at the other end of the table, their heads together, were a Bird, a Mouse, and a Sausage, each one wearing a crown, and each one's mouth forming a perfect 'o.'[43]

---

43   All of the above characters reference other well known Arcadian tales. Their provenance is at this time unknown. Which came first—*Snotty Saves the Day*, or the fairy tale characters? For an interesting speculation, see the forthcoming doctoral thesis, "Seaweed that Goes Pop and other Arcadian Heroic Figures," by Isabel Watson, Bel Regina College, Cockaigne. In it, this fine scholar draws on my own work, and that of Professor Joyanna Bender Boyce-Flood, to show that a partnership between the Reader and the Text results in changes in the physical world. Her work on the Centaur motif in the Maude Cycle (see Vale, year 22; Vale, year 26) is particularly noteworthy in light of the fact that a centaur-like being has been reported to be living in the northern

The Dog passed by on his way down the table. And the Dog's expression said, "Those are our allies."

"Oh," Snotty said. "I see."

Troubled, he remembered the Dead Things that fed the Great Lawn in the Garden of Earthly Delights. And by the look in the Dog's brown eyes, he knew that those had been the same as these. Allies, the Dog's eyes said. Comrades. Friends.

He thought about the Mexican piñatas he had shoveled into the dirt, and the puppies that had been buried, too. And he shuddered.

"Are you okay?" the Crimson Bear asked in a friendly way. Snotty nodded. But he found he wasn't hungry anymore, and when no one was looking, he pushed his plate aside. He tried his best to join in when he could. The rest of the company laughed and ate and drank and talked and ate some more. They all had a very good time, and Snotty wanted to have a good time, too. So while he may have been a little quiet, he tried his best to keep up his end of the conversation. It was only when the Bears looked away from him, laughing at some joke or other, that he let himself think back to those Dead Things buried in the Garden. And then it was as if a dark hand took hold of his heart and squeezed. But when the Bears looked back to see if he was enjoying himself, he did his best to smile.

Afterward, the Orange Bear showed him how to take charge of his bowl and spoon and cup, how to take them down to the Stream and wash them clean before stacking them with the others in neat piles at the edge of the meadow.

"Come and join me and my friends," the Orange Bear said, pointing to one of the campfires that had sprung up there. And Snotty, happy to be distracted from his own dark thoughts, agreed.

Around the fire sat the Crimson Bear and the Rose Pink Bear, a Robin's Egg Blue Bear, and a Lime Green Bear. The Orange Bear

mountains. A scientific expedition was planned to attempt contact, but, alas, the recent war has made travel impossible led Snotty over, and fetched them both mugs of hot cocoa with marshmallows melting in the middle, the same as the others had. For a moment, they all sat together, drinking these in silence. Then the Lemon Yellow Bear came over and sat down, too.

"Tell us a story," the Crimson Bear said to the Lemon Yellow Bear. "You know it's your turn."

At this, the Lemon Yellow Bear looked at Snotty, as if she was thinking over what story would be nicest for a guest.

"I think..." the Lemon Yellow Bear said, hesitating over her words—"I know I usually like to tell a happy story. But tonight I will tell you one that's sad."[44]

The other Bears looked at her with attention.

"Yes," the Lemon Yellow Bear said, and she gave a faint sigh. "Tonight I will tell you my story, by which I mean, how I came to be here with you. Because who knows how long we have to drink, and talk, and laugh together? If the Enemy overcomes us, all that will end."

The Crimson Bear straightened her back and poked at the fire.

"The Enemy will never win," she said. "Justice won't allow it."

"What Enemy?" Snotty wanted to say. He felt the Bears meant something other than the Gnomes—something bigger and more threatening still. But for now he drank his cocoa and was quiet.

"Once," the Lemon Yellow Bear began, "I lived in world that was more beautiful than I can remember without feeling sad."

---

44   Note: The Lemon Yellow Bear Story is a well-known Arcadian fairy tale of the oral tradition. This remains a rare written version. I believe this story to derive from the Megalopolitan oral tradition, from sources so ancient as to be impossible to trace. It may, in fact, be an exception to the general rule that there are no Megalopolitan fairy tales. I first remember hearing it told to the young Sophia by her nurse, a refugee from Megalopolis. But this source was uncertain as to where she had first heard the tale. We were all the more surprised when Professor Bender Boyce-Flood's translation of the *Legendus Snottianicus* revealed it in written form.

"I lived in a beautiful world too," said the Orange Bear with a reflective look.

"I did, too," said the Crimson Bear.

The Rose Pink Bear and the Robin's Egg Blue Bear nodded.

Snotty thought, "I lived in a world where there was nothing beautiful at all."

"In this world," the Lemon Yellow Bear went on, "I lived with a little girl. We lived in a small house, the neatest house you ever saw. Everything was small. Our animals were small and clever. Our flowers were small and had a beautiful smell. Our fruit and vegetables were small, and once you ate them you never forgot their taste. Everything was small, and perfect for its kind. And we were content there, with our small world, my little girl and I."[45]

For a moment the Lemon Yellow Bear was quiet. Then she went on:

"We would sit together for hours on the porch in two small chairs, watching the garden grow. Or we would go for walks, she and I, and look at the sky. There were always lots of birds flying there, birds who had come from other lands, and sometimes they would stop and tell us stories of the things they had seen. I've told you some of their stories, around this fire, other nights."

The Bears nodded. They remembered those tales with pleasure.

"We were very happy," the Lemon Yellow Bear said, and her red button eyes gleamed in the firelight.

The Bears nodded again. They had been happy in their worlds, too, Snotty saw. "But I," Snotty thought, "I don't think I was happy in my world. Not at all." And for the first time, this bothered him.

---

45   See analysis of this story, Prof. Joyanna Bender Boyce-Flood, *Storyland: Storehouse in the Ether?*, Otterbridge University Press, year 62, along with the theory of its biological fact. Professor Grayling has been particularly scathing about this theory, insisting that all physical law is based on the Law of the Strong. Yet Bender Boyce-Flood's conclusions seem to me irrefutable.

"One day a storm came from the North. The wind blew like a tornado for days; and from the clouds came ice crystals that were hard and jagged as glass. Nothing like this had ever been seen before—everyone went outside to look and catch the crystals in their hands.

"My little girl went too. Oh, I wish I'd stopped her! But how could I know? The Enemy had sent that storm, and in its ice crystals was the Fever of the Plains. And all who caught the crystals caught that disease as well."

All the Bears were silent with sympathy. Snotty couldn't help himself. He thought of Snowflake.

"When my little girl came back, she was changed," the Lemon Yellow Bear went on. "The Fever had hold of her: she hated everything small. She couldn't see beauty in our small animals, our small plants, our small house. Now she hated them because they were small. And because I was small, she hated me.

"Swearing I would find a way to help her, I set out on a quest. The storm had chased the birds away, and it was the birds I went in search of now. They would know the cure for this Fever, I thought. But when I found a bird—only one, all alone, faraway, blown off course—he told me that the birds would not be back to our world, and that the cure for the Fever could never be found there. He was sorry for me, he said, but it was best that I faced facts. And then he flew away.

"I made my way back home. I had been gone a long time, and my little girl had grown big. She hated small things—and me—more than ever before.[46] There was no place for me in her house, which was no longer small and cozy but was now big and grand. Crawling into a corner of one huge empty room in my grief, I found a small hole in the floor. I jumped inside and fell and fell and fell. And I landed here, to fight the Enemy who destroyed my world, or be destroyed myself in trying."

The Lemon Yellow Bear sipped her cocoa as the other Bears

---

46   The Law of the Small. See previous notes.

reflected on the tale. Even though it was a sad tale, Snotty saw they liked hearing it. Snotty liked hearing it, too. In fact, Snotty started to ask whether there were other stories like it, but the Rose Pink Bear said, "It's late." At this they all got up, trooped down to the Stream to wash their mugs, and then went to sleep in a big warm tent. Snotty went with them and found a bark bunk bed beside the Lemon Yellow Bear's. He was tired. It had been a long day.

"Night," the Lemon Yellow Bear said in sleepy voice. "Night," said the Rose Pink Bear and the Robin's Egg Blue Bear and the Orange Bear and the Lime Green Bear and the Crimson Bear.

"Night," Snotty said back. He was asleep almost before he finished the word.

———————

He woke sometime before dawn. Rolling over and peering at the Bears lying in their bunks in the dark, he could see a bit of the bright yellow plush of the Lemon Yellow Bear by the light of the night's last stars. The Lemon Yellow Bear murmured in her sleep and sighed.

Snotty got up. It was hard to get out of his warm bed, but something pushed him forward. He got up without disturbing his friends, and he went out, making his way to the tent where he could see Big Teddy sit, working by one lone light.

Chapter XIII

THE BATTLE DRAWS NEAR

In the big tent, Big Teddy stitched the sole of a red plush boot upended on a wooden form. There were plush boots of all sizes and colors, and in various stages of manufacture, hanging and lying about the tent.

Snotty walked from the doorway into the pool of light spread by Big Teddy's lamp and cleared his throat.

"Urrermph."

The big Bear looked up and, taking off her reading glasses, rubbed her snout in a tired way. But the look she gave Snotty was welcoming, and she waved one stubby and substantial black and yellow paw to show that Snotty should sit down on the chair beside her.

"Thank you," Snotty said.

They sat for a moment in silence. Big Teddy picked up her needle and went back to work. It was hard work for a Bear with such unwieldy paws, but Big Teddy made the most of it, as far as Snotty could see. He watched her for a while, and then he remembered he had something important he wanted to ask. There was something industrious and brisk about the Big Black and Yellow Bear that made you think she would be able to answer even the most difficult of questions.

"Big Teddy," Snotty began. Then a bowl sitting on the huge Bear's worktable caught his eye. It was filled with water. At the bottom of the water was a rose gold Key.

"My KEY!" Snotty said. So excited was he that, without thinking, he reached into the bowl and grabbed it tight.

A sound like the wind in a hurricane filled his ears. Then came the cries of a million birds and the flapping of their wings. The fabric of the tent disappeared, and Snotty could see far away.

He could see all the way home.

He could see everyone and everything. And he could see that same web from the top of the trees: the web that he, Snotty, was a part of.

He could see all of the worlds.

All of this happened faster than the time it's taken to describe it. Then Big Teddy stuck her paw in the bowl and took the Key away. It dropped back to the bottom with a faint 'clink.'

The world snapped back into place outside, and it was night in the tent again. Snotty sat there staring empty-eyed in front of himself for a long time.

Big Teddy looked at him in silence, a concerned expression on her black and yellow face.

Snotty, surprised, hiccupped and then belched. His eyes rolled back in his head, then went cross-eyed, then narrowed unpleasantly. He sat back in his seat, crossed his legs, put his hands together and formed a steeple with his fingers. From this position, he began to speak.

"You know, Big Teddy—and I'm only telling you this because I respect you, right?" he said. "I respect what you and your people have done here. I mean it, really. But between you and me..." Snotty leaned forward here in a confidential way. "I mean, how REAL is it? You've got to get involved, Big Teddy. Make a contribution. Engage yourself. You know what I'm saying, don't you. I could put you in touch with some guys, you know, consultants, like. Sure, they're Giant Garden Gnomes, and maybe those aren't your favorite kinds of people, but they know their business, and that's the important thing. It'd make all the difference in the world. Really. You should listen to me. I've been in this game for, hey, it must be two years now, and I know what I'm saying. And another thing..."

Snotty ranted on like this for a good while. When he showed no sign of stopping, the giant Bear looked around to make sure there was nothing sharp on the floor. With a heavy tread she stood. And then with an enormous paw she felled Snotty one more time.

This time, though, Snotty woke much faster, so it must have been a lighter blow than the first. The silly-looking Bear was back, standing next to Big Teddy. Both looked down at him in a worried way.

"All right now?" Big Teddy said. But Snotty was too confused to reply. He stood up, then sat down and tried to get his bearings. Big Teddy and the silly-looking Bear looked at him with silent sympathy.

"Sorry about that," Big Teddy said. "But with the Fever it's the only way."

"I understand," Snotty said. And to his surprise, he did. He was sick and that was the cure. It was perfectly clear. And that wasn't all. To his surprise, he understood many things now that he hadn't before.

It was like he had put on a pair of glasses and could see the world more plainly than before.

For example, he saw right away that the silly-looking Bear had a name. "I must've heard it, but I wasn't listening," he thought. "Of course. His name is Tuxton—Tuxton Ted. And those other Bears: the Orange Bear, the Rose Pink Bear, the Robin's Egg Blue Bear, the Lime Green Bear, and the Crimson Bear. They're called Tia, Fia, Fion, Mion, and Lui. The Lemon Yellow Bear's name, of course, is Melia. How could I have missed that before?"

Snotty wondered at this—at all of it. He looked at the bowl on the table and at the Key shining from its bottom. With a look of mistrust he said, "What IS that?"

Big Teddy and Tuxton Ted exchanged a look. "That's the Key," Big Teddy said. She paused as she considered how best to explain. "It's connected to all the other Keys, on each and every world." At Snotty's confused look, she tried again. "It's our connection to what Is."

"The height of Bear Technology," Tuxton Ted squeaked in his silly-sounding voice. "It took us hundreds of years to develop."

"I don't... I don't understand," Snotty said.

Big Teddy looked around the tent, as if for some kind of example. One massive paw massaged her jaw. Then she took up a large blank piece of paper.

On this paper she wrote the words: "TEDDY BEAR."

"Tuxton," she said quietly. "Please stand over there." Tuxton stood where Big Teddy pointed, across the table from Snotty.

Big Teddy pointed at the words. "This is what Tuxton is. Do you understand that?"

Snotty nodded. "Of course I do!" he said, vaguely irritated.

The Bear gave him a worried look. Then she wrote on the paper, "TUXTON TED." And she said, "This is Tuxton's name."

Snotty nodded again. He was getting annoyed. "They're treating me like a kid," he thought.

But Big Teddy wasn't finished. Now she drew a sketch on the paper, and this was a picture of Tuxton—a very good likeness, in fact.

"This is a picture of Tuxton," she said.

"Yes, I KNOW," Snotty said. But then, without warning, something in him shifted. He sat up, more alert now. "Okay," he said, intent. "I think I see."

Big Teddy, watching him, saw the shift. "Good," she said, nodding. "Now. Let me ask you a question. Think it over before you answer. "These things—" She pointed at the words and at the picture. "Are they Tuxton himself?"

"Of course not!" Snotty said. He moved uneasily in his seat. He sensed something important. But he didn't know what.

"Of course not," Big Teddy agreed. "Good, good. These things SAY Tuxton. But they're not Tuxton."

"No," Snotty agreed in turn. He felt excited.

"These things mean Tuxton, but they are not Tuxton. You can't store the meaning of Tuxton in this word"—here Big Teddy pointed at the word 'BEAR'—"or in this picture." She pointed to the portrait she had drawn. "We puzzled over this problem for many hundreds of years."

"Puzzled over what?" Snotty said. He was puzzled himself.

Big Teddy looked at Tuxton and rubbed her flat button eyes with her paws. Then she had an inspiration. She put her paw into the water of the bowl and pulled out the Key. She held this out to Snotty.

"Go on," she said in a gentle voice. "Don't grab it. Just touch one end. Now that it's out of the water the current won't be as strong."

Snotty looked doubtful. After what had happened, he was a little scared of the Key.

"Touch the Key and think of Tuxton," Big Teddy said. "And think: what does 'Tuxton' mean?"

Snotty hesitated. Then he reached out with two fingers and touched the Key. As he did, Tuxton told him his story:

"I am a very anxious bear [Tuxton said], and I have been that way my whole life. This is unusual for us Teddies; normally we're more easygoing than that. But I was born frightened, and that fear has never left me to this day.

"I don't remember much about being born. My first memory is of being shut in a dark box. I shouted and shouted and shouted, and pounded at the lid, but no one came. My first memories are terrifying ones. I hate to think about them, really. But it's always better to remember where you come from, because if you forget, you forget who you are, don't you? And if you forget who you are, what can you remember?[47]

---

47   This comment is of special interest, as it is similar in content to Dr. Malcolm Sivia's speculations on the problem of Arcadia's forgotten history, in *Connection: A Personal Journey of Discovery, Loss, and Love*, year 59. In that work, Dr. Sivia postulates that a culture has memory, the same as an individual. And that trauma affects that memory just as it does for an individual. The significance of this point is tremendous, and

"My next memory is of a blinding light. The lid of the box moved away, and I was in a bright white room. Later I learned this was a hospital, and I was brought there to do a job. My job was one I was well suited for, one in the medical profession. I was meant to comfort the small children in the wards, coax them to take their medicine, and keep them quiet at night.

"Of all the stuffed animals and dolls in that hospital I was the best at my job. That's something I'm proud of, but I can't take the credit for it. No, I was good at my job because I was so anxious. And because I was so frightened. Because of these things, I knew exactly how the children on my ward felt. I was able to comfort them in the way they wanted to be comforted, because it was the way I wanted to be comforted, too.

"It wasn't enough, though. I worked at it, but I always knew there was some terror still there that wouldn't go away no matter how hard I tried.

"One day a rumor came through the hospital. We were going to close! All of us, Bears, Dolls, Clowns, plastic Horses, none of us could believe it would happen. We worked harder than ever to prove the worth of the place. But it was no use. One day I lay still, comforting a child whose tonsils would have been better left where they were, and who'd been given orange juice by mistake after they'd been taken out. His throat hurt him, and he cried. He laughed when he saw my silly face, and he was quiet when I lay under his arm. The nurse said to him, 'Do you want to take that Bear home? We'll be closing soon, and if you don't he'll just get thrown away.'

"But the boy's mother hissed, 'Who knows what germs that thing's carrying?' And then she said to the boy, 'I'll buy you the biggest toy in

cannot be overstated. Professor Grayling's theory that Arcadia can remember nothing before the year 1 because of its loss of moral fiber through turning to the ideal of Happiness for All rather than Greatness for Some has little, other than the wishful thinking of its originator, to recommend it.

the hospital shop if you give up that Bear.'

"He wouldn't, though. He held me tight. But he had to sleep, and then they took me away. They put me, with all the other toys on my ward, in an even bigger box, and then they threw us all far away.

"Somehow, though, I could still hear that boy cry. He was crying for me, thinking it was his fault I was thrown away. I know he never forgot me, I know that for certain, for I've felt him since, with the Key. He is older now, with children of his own, but during the night he thinks of me, and all this time later, he still misses me. Of all the children I ever worked with, he is the child I think of most. He is why I'm here.

"I was terrified in that box, Snotty. But I remembered that little boy, and I thought if ever I got free of it I would try to find him again.

"A long time passed. Then the box we toys were in split open, on a smelly hillside, one day in the rain. I set out to find that little boy again. But I never did."

(Here Tuxton smiled his silly smile.)

"You look like that boy, Snotty, did you know that? I thought so the minute I saw you. And that makes me happy, somehow, and a little less frightened than before."

As Tuxton spoke, Snotty felt his story. He could feel Tuxton: where he came from, what it was like to be him. He could feel Tuxton's valor, his softness, his kindness, and his anxiety. He felt Tuxton himself. He understood that what was stored there in the Key WAS Tuxton. He understood that, if he practiced enough and was strong enough to stand it, he could understand the meaning of Tuxton. And that once he understood this meaning, he would never be able to look at the Bear in the same way again.

Snotty sat there. He frowned.

"I came to ask you a question," he said at last. Big Teddy nodded as if she'd known that all along.

Snotty held out his maimed right hand.[48] Even though it was starting to heal, his little finger's stump throbbed with pain. Tuxton and Big Teddy looked at it gravely. Snotty told them about the Bazaar and Aladdin's Cave, but they seemed to know the whole story already.

"Why did I do that?" he asked, troubled. "Why did I sell my little finger for a pile of trash?"

Big Teddy took up her pen one more time. On the paper she wrote the words, "Snotty's finger." Then she drew a picture of the missing finger. She pointed to the word, then to the picture. "You mistook your finger," she said, "for this... or for this."

"It's the Fever, Snotty," Tuxton squeaked. "The Fever makes it impossible to see what Is. You couldn't see that Trash was Trash because of it. You were ill."

"Aladdin told you it was treasure. You mistook the word for the thing."

"You mistook a word—'finger'—for your real finger," Tuxton explained. "As long as you didn't know what your finger was, it was a fair deal. A word traded for a word—that's a reasonable trade!"

"A thing traded for a thing," Snotty corrected him.

"But your finger isn't a thing," Big Teddy said. "Your finger is alive."[49]

---

48   As mentioned above, Lily the Silent's maimed hand was also her right one. See Fallaize, year 61, in particular his theory of reality formed by symbol. The more deeply I delve into *Snotty Saves the Day*, however, the more my meditations lead me to a more radical view.

49   This well-known section of *Snotty Saves the Day* deserves further research. (See Vale, year 54.) The concept of life being over-controlled by abstract thought, sometimes to deadly effect, is important to all branches of Arcadian thought. The Neofundamentalists, opposing this trend of research, state that the exact opposite is true: that Abstract Thought is the highest Good in Life, and all in Life should be sacrificed to its development. To which I can only reply: Can you eat Abstract Thought? Can you enjoy Abstract Thought more than the sun on your face on a summer day? And, most importantly, Can Abstract Thought restore the limbs, minds, and lives it

At this Snotty was quiet.

Without knowing he did it, Snotty picked up the pen. On the paper he wrote the word 'Snowflake.' Next to the word he drew an awkward sketch of the little horse. As Big Teddy and Tuxton watched, he pointed first to the word, then to the sketch, then into the air. His lips moved. But he said nothing.

"I don't understand," he said after awhile. The two Bears looked at him in silence.

Tuxton dug a paw into his plush pocket. "I brought you this," he said in his silly voice. And he held out a rose gold Key.

"My KEY!" Snotty said as he took it back. "Where did you find it?"

"Under the trees," Tuxton said. "I thought you'd want it."

Outside there was a sound. BOOM. BOOM. BOOM. Somewhere a siren began to wail. Snotty could hear Tia, Fia, Fion, Mion, and Lui shouting in the meadow outside. Melia appeared, breathless, in the door to the tent.

"They've found the Path," she said tersely. Big Teddy nodded, and Melia disappeared.

"What is it?" Snotty said. "What's that sound?"

"They're coming," Tuxton Ted said.

BOOM. BOOM. BOOM.

"No," Big Teddy said, and her voice was no longer gentle. "They're here."

"Yes," Tuxton said, as the rumbling grew louder. And Snotty saw he trembled. But the silly Bear steeled himself and went outside

The rumbling came closer. BOOM! BOOM! BOOM! Snotty was scared.

"Big Teddy," Snotty said urgently. "What do I do? Tell me what to do!"

But when he turned, Big Teddy was gone.

---

has destroyed in our recent civil war? Forgive me for bringing politics into an academic study. The times make it inevitable.

Chapter XIV

WAR

Outside, it was chaos.

Drums sounded with their dull thump from the Plains below. "Thurr-rrrump. Thurrr-rrrrump." That sound made the hair on the back of Snotty's neck stand on end.

And there was that rumbling, even closer than before: BOOM! BOOM! BOOM!

"What's happening?" Snotty shouted, running here and there. "What is it? What do I do now?" Melia, as she ran past with Tia, Fia, Fion, Mion, and Lui, said over her shoulder, "See you after the battle, Snotty." Her mouth trembled as she smiled.

"It's my turn to tell the next story, Snotty!" Lui called, and she blew him a kiss from her crimson paw. But Snotty saw her paw shake, and saw her steady it as she disappeared with the others down the rocky Path he had flown up with his Idea.

"Wait!" Snotty called after them. "Wait for me!" He ran after the Bears, but brought his foot down on the edge of a flat rock that skidded out from under him. His foot went one way, his ankle another, and a sharp pain made his teeth clench as he went over and down.

Nevertheless he hobbled on.

At the top of the Path the Dog stood, conferring with three figures. And Snotty saw these figures were the Monsters that he had refused to pardon in his glorious days as the Sun God.

"Is it you?" Snotty said. The Monsters looked completely different to him now. The Monstrous Woman was a large, startled Doll. The Tusked Boar was a worried Piglet with a runny nose. And the Polar

Bear was a white fluffy Teddy with a pink ribbon around his neck. He gave Snotty an anxious smile.

"Yes," the white Teddy said. "It's us."[50]

Snotty saw that the group circled something that bounced heavily on the ground. Coming closer, he saw it was an Idea. Only this Idea was more garishly colored than the others.

"What is it?" he said.

"It's a False Idea," the Doll said with a tight smile.

"How did it get here without an audience?" the Piglet squeaked. "A False Idea can't travel far on its own."

There was a moment of silence while everyone thought about what that meant. The Dog's expression said, "No. It hasn't come here on its own. And there are more to follow."

A black shadow covered them. Looking up, Snotty saw a Dragon flying overhead.

"Is that...?" he said. Then he stopped, ashamed. The Dog nodded grimly. Yes, it was the Dragon Snotty had pardoned. It had joined the Gnomes as their advance guard.

"It's not your fault," the Piglet squeaked consolingly. "You couldn't have known."

"Everything looks different when you have the Fever," said the

---

50 Transformation of frightening creatures into helping ones is a common motif in Arcadian tales, past and present. An interesting contrast with Megalopolitan literature, where this only occurs in very early bardic epics. (See *Catalog of the ANALECTA ARCADIA and the ACTA ARCADIA*, compiled by Prof. Joyanna Bender Boyce-Flood, Otterbridge University, Year 76.) More recent Megalopolitan stories focus on the triumph of the hero over frightening characters ("Anthony Saves the World" is the most characteristic of these), while Arcadian stories ("Reine the Fox" and countless others) trace a transformation of frightening characters into helpful ones, through the agency of a character, or characters, greeting the monsters with wary compassion. See the Maude Cycle, and the stories of Maude's friendship with Death. Death, in these tales, is a beautiful woman in the full bloom of middle age, with a deep concern for the good of all living things. Quite different from the monster Death of Megalopolis.

fluffy white Bear.

They all looked at Snotty with sympathy as he hung his head. The fluffy Bear patted him on the arm.

"The Dragon never could have joined us anyway," the Doll said. "Dragons hate to look small. They can't live without thinking they're Big and Strong."

"But the Dragon IS Big and Strong," Snotty said, astonished. The others looked back at him, just as surprised.

"Nobody's as Big and Strong as they look," the Doll said matter of factly. "I thought everyone knew that."[51]

"But... but...," Snotty stammered, not knowing what to say. To cover his confusion, he kicked at the False Idea as it spun and sputtered on the ground. "What do we do with THAT?" he said.

The Doll pulled him back. "Don't touch it," she said. "If it doesn't get attention, it'll die on its own."

The Dog agreed with this and turned to lead them all away.

BOOM. BOOM. BOOM. The dull noise filled the air. But Snotty couldn't see where it came from.

He hurried after the others, but the pain in his ankle made it hard for him to keep up. "Wait!" he said, and the Piglet, who was just in front of him, turned around. "What Idea was that, anyway?"

"That?" the Piglet said in its worried way. "That Idea is called Only the Strong Survive."[52]

"Oh," Snotty said. The pain in his ankle got worse. He had to stop.

---

51   A well-known Arcadian folk saying, and one that I recall, from personal conversation, always particularly irked Professor Grayling, who insisted it only showed the stupidity of the masses.

52   This dialogue is obscured by pen markings in the copy of *Snotty Saves the Day* found in the queen's library after her death. Reconstructed from translation of the *Legendus Snottianicus*. (See *Legendus Snottianicus: translations of fragments of an Arcadian folk tale*, translated by Prof. Joyanna Bender Boyce-Flood, Otterbridge University Press, year 34.)

BOOM. BOOM. BOOM.

The sky turned red now, filling the air with an eerie light. Smoke from the Plains rose up and blotted out the sky. The creatures broke into a run, following the Teddy Bears heading in a grim stream down the mountain. Snotty sprinted to keep up, but came down again on his hurt ankle. He fell with a little cry. He pulled himself up painfully, but it was no use. For now he couldn't go on.

As he watched, helpless, the Teddy Bear Brigade marched down the Mountain to War. A trio of stiff Brown Bears with matching tartan bows around their necks ran by, holding rifles at a diagonal against their plush brown chests. The Dog, leading a platoon of brightly colored Kites, disappeared down the mountain's side. Melia marched behind the Girl Bear Cadre, shouting orders to Tia, Fia, Fion, Mion, and Lui as they went. And Tuxton, silly-looking as ever, but with a grim, determined expression on his silly face, brought up the rear.

"Tuxton!" Snotty called. But in the hubbub, the Bear couldn't hear. "Tuxton! Wait!"

Snotty tried to run after his friend, limping past the marching groups as they formed and followed the others to the battlefield. Beads of perspiration appeared on his forehead and dripped down his face. He put up his hand to wipe these away. A fierce wind began to blow.

Snotty lost sight of Tuxton in the crowd that streamed out of the Teddy Bear Camp. Then, just when he had given up hope, he spotted the Bear standing alone at the edge of the meadow. Tuxton's head was bent. He murmured a few words to himself. Snotty struggled to get to him, but the Bear was too far away. And there was something more. Something pulled at Snotty's ankle. Something that hurt.

Looking down, Snotty saw it was the False Idea. It was caught on the edge of his purple plush boots. It was the Idea that slowed him down.

Frustrated, Snotty tried to shake it off, but it clung to his bad ankle, and the movement only caused more pain. He jammed his hands in his pockets and gritted his teeth as the pain washed over him.

To his surprise, he now heard Tuxton speak—as clear as if the Bear had spoken right in his ear.

Snotty had forgotten the Key. But he touched it now with his damp hands. And he could feel again what Tuxton was and what Tuxton felt.

Tuxton said a prayer. And Tuxton's prayer was this: "I know that I am only a silly-looking stuffed Bear and that silly-looking stuffed Bears are not meant to fight. I know that I am going to lose and that everyone I know and love will lose with me. But now I am going to fight for one reason: because someone has to. And there is no one left but us who will."

That was what Tuxton prayed as he stopped by the edge of the Teddy Bear meadow, and offered up his one prayer to the hugeness of the Universe. What Tuxton prayed for was not Triumph, but Justice.[53]

And then, shouldering his weapon, he joined the creatures pouring down the mountainside.

"TUXTON!" Snotty shouted. His words blew back at him on the hot wind. "TUXTON! WAIT!" Of course Tuxton couldn't hear. He marched on, and in a moment he would disappear over the rise.

Snotty hobbled after him as fast as he could go. The Idea flapped behind him. Snotty grabbed at it, and it let go of his foot, grasping now onto the plush of his arm.

"TUXTON!" Snotty yelled again, trying to go faster still. He followed the Bear over the rise. BOOM, BOOM, BOOM, he could hear. But when he got to where he could look down the mountain, he found he was alone. Snotty realized that he was on another path, one different than the one he had come up before. This path was

---

53   This section also blacked out in the copy-text; it is reconstructed from the *Legendus Snottianicus*. See above note.

lonely and straight and covered with fine white rock. It was the only way down. Gritting his teeth against the pain, he started down its pale slope.

"WAIT!" he wailed, but there was no one there to hear. He could still hear that sound. BOOM. BOOM. BOOM. He headed for that, when something jumped out and grabbed him.

"Acckk!" Snotty shrieked as the Thing tackled him, wrestling him to the ground. "Get off! Leave me alone!" He punched at the Thing, and the Thing punched back. Wrapping his fingers around the Thing's throat, he choked it. But the harder he choked it, the harder he found it himself to breathe.

"What are you DOING?" he gasped. And the Thing gasped back. That was when Snotty saw its face. And he saw the Thing was him, too. It was Snotty. He was wrestling with his Self.

So stunned at this was Snotty, and so frightened, that he let go, falling with a bump onto the rocky Path. His Self fell back, too, and sat there, staring.

"Let me go!" Snotty said, but his voice sounded sulky, even to him. His Self didn't answer. It just rubbed its neck where Snotty had tried to throttle it and gave him a reproachful look.

"Look," Snotty argued. "I have to get down there. I have friends in trouble."

"I'm not stopping you," Snotty's Self said in a hurt-sounding voice.

But when Snotty tried to stand and walk down the Path, his Self tackled him and wrestled him to the ground again.

"Erm! Urmph! URRRPP!" Snotty gasped as the two rolled and kicked at each other. The False Idea gibbered and squeaked, still clinging to Snotty's arm. And Snotty saw another Idea clutching at his Self's chest. It was the Idea that had kidnapped him from the Fortress of the Gnomes. But he didn't recognize it.

"Just STOP, why don't you?" Snotty shouted, frustrated that he couldn't get his own Self to obey. Instead his Self gave him a final push, and they went tumbling into the wood next to the Path, where they landed under a tall tree.

"OOOHHPPPHHH," Snotty said as his Self fell hard against him. It crushed the False Idea between them right up against Snotty's face. "AAARRRPPHHH!" he said. With the False Idea smooshed there, it was hard to breathe.

The two of them, Snotty and his Self, rolled around and around, in a well-matched tangle. As Snotty huffed and puffed and tried to get on top, he saw, over his Self's heaving shoulder, Big Teddy. She stood at the top of the white stone Path. Snotty tried to call out, but his words were lost in the tangle with his Self.

Big Teddy scanned the mountain looking for something or someone, and she didn't see Snotty as he lay there, struggling with his Self. Instead she looked at the sky. There was a shriek from above. Snotty saw the Dragon flying hard overhead.

"LOOK OUT!" Snotty tried to yell. But the False Idea squirmed against his mouth and crushed the words before they could get out.

"EERRRUUUMMMPPPHHH!" Snotty wailed, helpless. He watched the Dragon spit out little gray jagged stones—Dragon's Teeth.[54] As they hit the ground, a thicket sprang up. Its twisting branches were tangled, thorny, and mean, and they threatened to cut off Big Teddy from the Plains and her fellows below. But a white figure leapt over the growing thicket's top, landing at the Bear's stubby plush feet. It was a little white horse, and it knelt so that Big Teddy could awkwardly mount.

"SNOWFLAKE!" Snotty wailed, tearing the False Idea from his chest. Snowflake and Big Teddy turned his way. Snotty could see that Snowflake's wound was healed. It had left a little silver nub between

---

54   See *An Elegant Theory of the Contiguity of Theater Arts and Neurobiology*, Dr. Chloe Watson, Otterbridge University Press, year 14, appendix: "Dragon's Teeth, the Donatee Mountains, and Early Arcadian Theater: A Sketch."

his eyes.

BOOM. BOOM. BOOM. The hideous sound called again. And Big Teddy and Snowflake, losing no time, wheeled around. The thicket was growing—heaving and twisting fast. Another moment and it would be too late. Backing up, Snowflake reared, pressing back on his flanks and sprang up. And just as the wall of dark wood leapt up, he leapt too, just that much farther, and cleared it before it shut out the sky.

BOOM. BOOM. BOOM.

The black shadow of the Dragon passed overhead. Snotty was alone. And the wall of thorns between himself and his friends reached all the way to the sky, blotting out the sun.

Chapter XV

THE TOP OF THE WORLD

It would be nice to say that this upset our hero. But the truth is at the bottom he was relieved. There was no way he could join the battle now. No one could expect him to get over that wall.

"That's a magic wall," he said to his Self, who was busy kicking the False Idea. "Nothing I can do about that, is there? Not my fault it grew up."

Snotty's Self was silent.

Snotty had the feeling he should at least try to get over the wall. So he attempted to climb. But whatever branches he managed to get his foot on just collapsed under his weight. Annoyed, he grabbed at a branch overhead. A large thorn went through the base of his maimed finger, and bright red blood spurted out.

He jumped back, sucking on the wound, but the blood wouldn't stop. So at first he didn't notice the dozens of small animals running down the thicket from the Tree Canopy above.

Then he heard the screeching of the Dragon.

All the animals of the trees fled from the sound: the frogs and the beetles and the caterpillars and the crickets and the pale pink shrimps and the blind white newts. A violet and blue Dragonfly fluttered in front of Snotty before darting for cover. And Snotty recognized the little pink Crab who had helped him find his Key. It recognized him, too, and scuttled up his arm, where it quivered with fear against his neck.

Again the black shadow of the Dragon passed overhead.

The Dragon enjoyed its work. It enjoyed seeing, with its sharp eye, the terror it caused in the smaller, weaker creatures down below. It took now to diving from the sky and plucking animals from the ground. With a writhing lizard or a terrified weasel in its claws, it would soar upward, letting the animal drop to the hard earth below.

Snotty, caught up in the general panic, ran with the others, forgetting for now the sharp pain in his ankle. The Crab clung to his neck, its tiny pink claws dug into his skin. The next thing Snotty knew, bigger claws dug into his back. "Hey!" he yelled as he lifted off the meadow floor.

"Close your eyes," the Crab said in his ear, and Snotty knew this was good advice. He closed his eyes. He went higher and higher into the air. He could hear the flapping wings of the Dragon. Higher and higher they flew.

It began to snow.

Fat flakes landed on the back of Snotty's neck, first slow, then fast enough to form a thick white sheet. He hoped the Crab was all right. He could feel it pinching still at the base of his neck, so he thought it was.

Frozen with cold and breathing hard in the thin air, Snotty didn't feel it when the Dragon let him go. He didn't fall so much as tumble, and he was surprised that he didn't have far to go. To his relief, he collapsed onto solid ground, a rocky outcropping of some sort. Or so he thought. It was hard to tell. The snow fell in thick sheets, and he and the Crab—who still clung to his skin—were soon covered with the stuff.

As the snow fell and covered them, the cold disappeared, and it seemed to a drowsy Snotty that he was wrapped in a blanket that was soft and warm. "This IS nice," he murmured, pleased. And, shutting his eyes again, leaning back against a snowy mound, Snotty forgot who and where he was.

The snow covered his face. Snotty slept.

Later the snow stopped. Snotty's nose twitched from under a

clean white curtain of snow. The Crab's claw appeared, waving, as it dug its way out, and then came the Crab itself, clinging by a pincer to a lock of Snotty's hair. It looked at Snotty, then, reaching out, it pinched. Hard.

Snotty frowned. From somewhere in the deep, delicious hole he had fallen into, he could feel the pinch. But he refused to move.

The Crab considered this. Then it began to dig. It dug a burrow down to Snotty's side, and when it got there, it followed a trail of blood to his maimed finger. Taking hold of the base of the wound in one claw, it pulled tight.

"YOW." Snotty's eyes shot open. He sat up, sending showers of powdery snow in all directions.

The Crab held on. Snotty shook his hand. "Ow! Get off! Let go!" he yelled. But only when the Crab was sure that Snotty was wide awake did it let go and fall back to the snow below.

Snotty shook his hand and sucked at it. He looked up—the air had cleared and he could see all around. He looked again. He caught his breath. He thought—no, he was sure—no, it couldn't be—no, it was.

He was sitting on the Top of the World.

A light wind blew thin wisps of cloud in the now cold blue sky. There was nothing up where he was but air and cloud, and when Snotty looked down, mountains stretched out beneath him toward the plains. Snotty was at the top of the tallest peak.

"Where am I?" he wondered, excited, all pain forgotten now. "Is this the Peak of Transcendence?"

He looked around, though, and saw it couldn't be. Because there, hanging off to the right, was the Peak of Transcendence itself. It was white. It was pure. It was unattainable.

It was under him.

"That's impossible," Snotty muttered. "The Peak of Transcendence is the highest Peak there is! Everyone knows that." He shook his head, confused. Did everyone know that? Who said so? Who said that the

Peak of Transcendence was the highest peak there was? Because, well, obviously it wasn't. "THIS is the highest peak there is! Only, I don't know its name."[55]

This troubled Snotty for a moment, until he remembered he could name the peak himself. The idea comforted him a little. Investigating further, Snotty found he was balancing precariously on a promontory jutting out over a sharp slope of big white rocks. Still exploring, and trying to figure out what to name this place, he brushed off the remaining snow and, standing upright, looked cautiously ahead.

He could see far out over the Plains. A thin blue column of electricity appeared at the edge of a far off Sea, dancing along the horizon there.

"Hey," Snotty said, distracted. "What's that?" He took a step forward to get closer to the beautiful blue light. And even though it was so far away, Snotty could hear it call to him.

"BBBBZZZZZTTTTTT."

Snotty rubbed his eyes and shook himself, but when he opened his eyes again, the thin blue column was still there.

"BBBBZZZZZTTTTT."

"It IS calling me," Snotty thought, excited.

"BBBZZZZTTTTTTT."

It was. It was calling him.

With a dreamy smile on his face, Snotty put out his arms as if to hug the column, which snaked up and down the shores of the faraway Sea. Snotty took a step toward it onto a jutting rock.

Snotty took another step. Then another. Then another.

---

55   Selective blindness in heroes is a common motif in Arcadian tales. See Sivia, year 59, for a groundbreaking discussion of selective blindness in culture. Dr. Sivia shows that an individual *can only see what he believes to be true.* Only Love, he argues, can open the individual's eyes to what is the actual physical world. And as goes the individual, so goes culture. I cannot emphasize this point enough—though recent assassination attempts indicate others in the opposition find it enough and more!

His left foot moved forward into the air above the rocky, snow-dusted slope below. He was about to step into the void when a loud whooshing sound startled him. He looked down and saw what he was about to do. Losing his balance, he teetered first forward then backward. Up above, blocking the pale gold sun, was an enormous white bird.[56] The wind made by the flapping of its wings reached Snotty, pushing him backward just enough so he could recover his balance. And with that, he threw himself back onto the ledge and grabbed hold of a leathery root growing there.

He lay there breathing hard, afraid of what he had almost done. Shuddering, he shoved his hands into his pockets. When he did, he touched the Key. And when he pulled himself up, propping himself against a rock and looking out at the landscape again, everything was changed.

The blue column was gone. Instead, the whole world spread out in front of Snotty. The whole of the world was at War. And he could feel it all.

"No!" Snotty cried out. "I don't want to know!"

"Too bad," the Key said as Snotty shoved it back in his pocket. "Too late now."

And it was. He couldn't stay there forever, could he? He searched the horizon for the thin blue light. He was sure that it would tell him what to do. But it was gone now. All that was left was the War.

Snotty took a deep breath and tested his bad ankle. It still hurt, but that didn't matter much anymore. Now he knew what he had to do. There was no doubt about it at all. He lowered himself down the side of the mountain, onto the steep rocky slope below.

As he skidded down the slope, he remembered the little pink

---

56   Again, a common motif in Arcadian legend, even in recent formations. It is said, for example, that on the day of Lily the Silent's death, an enormous white bird was seen taking her soul away over the Donatee Mountains. (Personal conversation with Sophia the Wise.) For further discussion, see Fallaize, year 61.

Crab. Snotty scrambled back, though his ankle throbbed and the pain made him sick to his stomach. When he got back to the ledge on top, he scooped up the Crab and put it back on his shoulder. And then he hurried, as fast as he could, ignoring the pain that shot up his leg, back down toward the Plains.

Chapter XVI

MEANWHILE, ON THE PLAINS OF DESOLATION

The battle was a horrible one. It was a massacre, the Big slaughtering the Small without mercy. The Bardic Gnome, platinum wreath on his brow, watched from a distant butte as the battle unfolded, contemplatively plucking a string on his lyre. "It will make another episode in the epic of the Gnomes," he thought. And there and then he wrote that great epic poem, "The Slaughter of the Small," composed on the battlefield for the greater Glory and future Fame of the Gnomes. Here it is in its entirety:

> There are much nobler sports than those that catch
> At niggling little irritating gnats
> And crush them underfoot as we go on
> To Gnomish Fame and Glory on our Lawn!
>
> The battle was beneath us, that's a fact
> But 'long as we do win is the main act
> No Rebels can oppose our giant maw
> If only they weren't stuffed, we'd eat them raw!
>
> (refrain) Hah, hah, hah, hah! Hah, hah, hah, hah! Ha-HA!
>
> Now listen, younger Gnomes, unto our tale
> Of how we strove to reach our snowy Grail
> The Sun God did rise up as was foretold
> And snuck into the Rebel Camp so bold

He found his way upon the Path of Care
That scrubby track that leads to Rebel Lair
We followed him with all our derring-do
To slaughter and wipe out that motley crew!

The Rebels had no choice but stand and fight
How stupid to oppose our awful might!
Those mis'rable Girl Bears, we trussed their paws
And shot a few more martyrs for the cause!

(repeat refrain) Hah, hah, hah, hah! Hah, hah, hah, hah! Ha-HA!

There was one Bear who lived to fight again
She rose up and, determined, bit our man
Who shooed her like an insect on his hand
And stomped her till she smothered in the sand.

The black and yellow Teddy rode her steed
Into the midst of Gnomes she gave the lead
To Fairy Tale Creatures, big and small
I tell you, Gnomes, we just destroyed them all!

Those Pleasures Living and those Pretty Toys
We never had such fun in killing joys!
Although it was beneath us, it's the truth
That Gnomes delight in being without ruth!

(repeat refrain) Hah, hah, etc.

And let us not forget the noble Dog
Alone among the rabble did us jog

To feelings of good will and brotherhood
His stand with trash can ne'er be understood

He snarled at us and ran into the fray
A flamethrower just blew him all away
Big Teddy then was left without a shield
We broke her pony's knees until he yield'd

And gloating then we finished up our game
We pulled the Bear to pieces all the same
Made sure her parts were scattered on the Plain
So never will she e'er be whole again

We won, we won, we won, we're proud to say
Tomorrow will there dawn a Gnomish Day
With Gnomish rights and many Gnomish laws
And no one left to tell us of our flaws!

(repeat refrain ad infinitum until drunk or asleep)

There was no epic poem left by the Bears. They left no words. There was nothing left at all.[57]

All that was left was the Wind as it screamed across the desolation of the Plains. The Wind bore the pieces of Big Teddy away. And howled over the lifeless battlefield.

---

57   Except, of course, for the testimony of this tale.

Chapter XVII

A DOOMED ATTEMPT

As Snotty ran from the Top of the World, he forgot everything but getting down to where the battle raged. He ran through meadows, and he ran through streams, and he ran through thickets, and he ran down boulder-strewn slopes. His ankle hurt him, but he didn't care. He ran.

He'd forgotten, too, the wall of thorny branches. There it was now, rising up, dark green and impenetrable between him and the Plains.

Snotty threw his body at the wall, and the Crab hacked at it with its claws, but it was no use. Snotty stared at its tangled green mass.

"Excuse me," said a voice behind him. He twisted around. The pain in his ankle made him wince.

There was a Handsome Prince seated on a tall black horse. Snotty assumed this was a Handsome Prince, anyway, from his expensive clothes and self-confident air. As it turned out, he was right.

"I wonder if you could help me," the Prince said in a suave voice. "I am trying to find a Damsel in Distress. She is... er..." The Prince pulled a piece of parchment from a red velvet tunic and read from it. "She is located on the Top of the World, and, er, it says here she's in disguise. Damned irregular, really," he said in a disapproving tone. "Of course, once I've saved her, we'll put a stop to that."

"What?" said Snotty, who stared at an efficient looking sword hanging from the Prince's belt.

"Yes. She needs to be rescued, apparently, and, of course, that's my business. After which I'll marry her, take her home, put her in charge of my castle, and give her lots of pretty clothes and so on. You know the kind of thing I mean. In return, the deal is she'll admire me and encourage others to admire me every hour of the day. That's fair, I think."

The Prince looked at Snotty anxiously.

"Un-huh," Snotty said, still looking at that sword. "Listen, I don't mean to be rude. But give me your sword, would you?"

"Certainly not!" the Prince said, offended. "I need it."

But Snotty really wanted that sword.

"Lend me your sword," he suggested casually. "Come on. It's not doing you any good just hanging there, is it?" The Prince looked at him doubtfully. "Look," Snotty coaxed, "Just let me have it for a little while, okay?" Then he had an inspiration. "Give me the sword, and... and...and I'll tell you where the—er... What did you call her?"

"The Damsel."

"The Damsel. Right. Hand it over and I'll tell you where the Damsel is. Can't be fairer than that, can I?"

The Prince eyed him suspiciously. "You know where she is?"

"Yeah, yeah," Snotty said. "The Top of the World. She's sitting up there in the snow. Just above and to the right of the Peak of Transcendence over there." He put his maimed hand into his pocket and held his breath.

"Oh yeah?" the Prince said. "If you really know where she is, tell me her name." At this, Snotty, taking a deep breath, clutched the Key.

"Her name," Snotty said, "is Lily."[58]

---

58 A common Arcadian name, as well as that, of course, of Arcadia's first known queen, Lily the Silent. The name also frequently appears as that of a secondary character in Megalopolitan tales, usually the housemaid, the laundress, or the concubine. (Examples of this are found in such Megalopolitan classics as "Lindsay the Center of the World," in which a thin Megalopolitan girl coaxes an uncle into giving her a larger dowry than she needs; "What Shall We Say to the Doctor?" in which a thin Megalopolitan girl persuades a doctor to turn her into the most beautiful girl in the

"That's it!" the Prince said, excited. "Here's the sword. Show me the path to the Damsel!" He unbuckled his belt and handed it down. Snotty didn't bother to thank him. He just lifted the sword up and slashed at the brush, which melted away at its touch.

"Follow the path behind me," Snotty shouted over his shoulder as he hacked his way deeper and deeper into the hedge. "There should be drops of blood all the way down."

"Is she very beautiful?" the Prince called out after him. But Snotty, almost all the way through, didn't answer. The Prince shrugged, then turned and followed the path that Snotty had advised.

As for Snotty, he broke through the last remaining branch, and the Crab, giving his neck one last pinch for luck, disappeared into the brush. Snotty's heart beat fast and his ankle throbbed as he looked down the mountainside to the battlefield. He dreaded what he would find. But, strapping the sword onto his little body, he set off down the slope, at as fast a pace as he could manage on the slippery rock.

———————

Over the Plains, the sky darkened with blowing dust and sand and grit. No movement was to be seen except, here and there, a rogue Gnome or two, separated from the main army, looting the piles of massacred Bears.

One such Rogue Gnome snuffled and snorted as he threw the carcasses aside, yanking off what shirts and hats and tiny weapons he could find. It gave him pleasure, wading through the heaps of corpses and kicking them aside after stealing his souvenirs. So much pleasure, in fact, that he failed to notice he had, in his frenzy, uncovered a moving paw. That paw waved weakly from beneath another body as he prowled past. And the Gnome didn't notice when the paw pushed

land; and "The Golden Glove," in which a thin Megalopolitan girl finds a magic glove that enables her to marry a rich older husband. See Vale, year 22.)

the Teddy Bear body above it aside, or when a half-dead Tuxton dragged himself up to the dust-clogged air.

Pulling himself out, Tuxton saw that his best plan was to make for the boulders at the foot of the Mountains of Resistance. Ducking and crawling, this was what he did. He tried not to look, as he passed, at the limp and contorted faces of his comrades as he used them for cover to hide him from the Gnome. He was almost dead, though, and, worse, his spirit was wounded to death. He had no real chance of escape.

The Gnome saw him and leapt, grabbing hold of him. He tried his best to twist Tuxton's neck.

The little Bear fought back with a fury that took the Gnome by surprise. There was a loud and horrible ripping noise, and the Gnome, his eyes bugging out with shock, went down. A tiny dagger stuck in his gut. Tuxton, one paw held to his face against the swirling of the dust and grit, used all his strength to yank the dagger out. A gush of green guts and vapor came with it. Tuxton wrapped a bandanna around his face against the foul smell and staggered toward the Mountains.

The sounds of the gloating, looting Gnomes followed him as his stubby legs pounded the desert floor. He ran as fast as he could for the cover of the rocks.

The Wind howled louder and louder and stronger and stronger, and Snotty had to struggle hard against it as he came skidding down the Path.

It was here that he met Tuxton, bandanna still wrapped around his face, fighting his way up the mountain.

"Tuxton!" Snotty cried out, but his voice was sucked into the Wind and blown away. It was impossible to speak, so the two friends fell on each other, exhausted. Tuxton leaned against Snotty, panting gently.

Snotty pulled him behind a rock, sheltering them from the Wind. "Tuxton, what's happened?" he said, trying to keep the fear from his voice. Then, when Tuxton didn't answer, he spoke in alarm: "What's wrong? Why don't you answer?"

Snotty held Tuxton by the shoulders and looked into his silly eyes. These eyes looked back with a message of the kind no one would want to hear.

Slowly and gently, Snotty untied the bandanna from around Tuxton's face.

There was no face left. Tuxton's muzzle with its silly tongue had been ripped away by the Gnome. There was nothing but a void of white stuffing left behind.

Tuxton's eyes met Snotty's and held them there.

"Melia?" Snotty said finally. "Tia? Fia? Fion, Mion, and Lui?"

Tuxton shook his head.

Snotty swallowed hard. "The Dog?" he said. "And... and... Big Teddy?"

At this, Tuxton's silly eyes filled with tears. The tears ran over and down his brown plush cheeks.

And Snotty hurled himself against the Wind down the Path toward the Plains. Tuxton pushed himself from the boulder to follow. But he had spent all his strength in the upward climb, and now he fainted dead away.

Snotty struggled on down below. He passed his Self on the Path. It whispered, "Where's your friend?" And Snotty realized that he had, in his rush, left Tuxton behind. Now he turned and retraced his steps until he found the unconscious Bear.

Holding him, Snotty gave Tuxton Ted a gentle shake. The Bear woke just enough to find the strength to cling to Snotty's neck.

And Snotty, with Tuxton clutched to his chest, negotiated the last steep and rocky path down to the desert plain alone.

The Wind screamed.

Chapter XVIII

ALL IS LOST

On the desert plain, the Wind blew hard enough to knock a boy down.

The gold sand it kicked up covered the whole of the desert. What had been a battlefield was lost in blowing sand.

Snotty, Tuxton still clinging to his chest, struggled through the sand, which was as deep and shifting as fresh fallen snow. He shouted against the Wind.

"BIG TEDDY! BIIIGGG TTTEEEDDDDDDDDYYYYY!"

There was no answer, of course. Snotty staggered on a yard or so more, but the wind and the sand were too much for him. Soon he couldn't go any farther. Snotty and Tuxton collapsed slowly onto the desert floor.

The Wind howled. The sand buried them both. Only Snotty's mouth was left, gasping, above it.

The sky turned darker and darker, and then there was no more light at all.

All was lost.

Chapter XIX

A ROYAL FEAST

After the darkness came the dawn. It always does.

The desert plain was empty now. And still. The Wind disappeared as if it had never been. The landscape, as far as the eye could see (if there had been an eye to see), was covered with a thin coat of fine gold sand.

If there had been a battle here, a massacre, some bloody and infernal deed, it was now so buried, so covered in the sands of Time, as to have lost all meaning. Now it was no more (if it had ever been any more) than a faintly remembered dream.

There was a dreamer, though. There was Snotty, snoring through his sand-crusted mouth, heaving uneasily in his sleep.

Windmilling his arms while asleep, flailing against some enemy, Snotty had worked his way free of the sand. He lay there now on the desert floor, warmed by the balmy early hours of the day. His nose twitched at a newly risen light breeze. He gave a gasping snort before turning over on his side.

In the eastern sky, the morning star shone clear as a jewel. The sky cradling it blushed and deepened and turned to light.

As the day came forward, the star, instead of making way, clung with stubborn pride to its place in the sky. Instead of fading it shone even brighter than before. And it made a clear, high sound. "BBBBBBBZZZZZZZTTTTTT."

Snotty smiled in his sleep, hiccupped, and snored on.

The star, attracted by the child, moved closer in the sky. Closer and closer it came, shining ever brighter, until it loomed over Snotty, casting over him a silver light. Then that silver light narrowed, extended, and glowed blue, until a blue column glowed right over Snotty's sleeping head.

"BBBBZZZZTTTTT."

For a moment the light hovered there. Then the blue column slid with an easy movement to the desert floor, where it unzipped— "zzziiippp!"—from top to bottom. And from inside the column of glowing light stepped the most beautiful young man in the world.

Snotty slept on. His forehead wrinkled, though, as if something in his dream had changed.

The young man was cool and elegant and strong. His eyes were a clear, deep turquoise. His hair was glossy black, his teeth pearlescent, his nose straight, his skin a burnished white. His dress was of an understated magnificence that couldn't be ignored.

Elegance was the hallmark of everything the beautiful young man said or did.

As the column of blue light rolled up and disappeared behind him, the young man stood there, reflecting in the dawn. His long, patrician fingers tapped at his well-formed chin. He gazed down at Snotty, and his look was one of perplexity and concern.

"Dear, dear," he murmured as he bent down protectively to flick some sand from the child's face. "Dear, dear."

Snotty, snorting and coughing and choking on swallowed bits of sand, sat bolt upright and stared. It was as if he had woken from a bad dream. As indeed he had.

"Wha...wha...where...," Snotty said. He remembered something from somewhere and felt blindly around himself in the sand. "Tuxton!" he shrieked. "Tuxton, where are you? TUXTON!"

He was still only half awake when he scrabbled frantically in the sand, tearing at his hands. The young man watched him. His look was full of sorrow.

Snotty was almost hysterical now. He jumped up and screamed,

"Tuxton! Big Teddy! Melia! Snowflake! WHERE ARE YOU?"

Swift as a breeze, the young man was at Snotty's side, his arm around the child's shoulders, shaking him gently.

"Ssssh," he said soothingly. "It was only a bad dream. Sssshhh."

At first Snotty refused to be comforted. He turned wildly this way, then that. He saw the beautiful young man. "You!" he said eagerly. "Maybe you know. My friends. Where have my friends gone?"

The beautiful young man touched Snotty's chin with his long fingers and gave him a rueful look. "There, there," he murmured again. "It must have been a nasty one, your dream. But you're awake now." When Snotty looked at him, confused, he explained. "A dream. It was only a bad dream."

Snotty rubbed his eyes with his fists and took in the scene around him: the majestic, pure, and empty desert. He shook his head and rubbed his eyes again. But when he opened them, it was still the same. The golden sand lying glistening in the early morning sun, under the triangular glory of the Peak. The empty desert, the white Peak and the beautiful young man.

"Better now?" the young man inquired. "All right?"

Snotty blinked. The young man looked familiar. "Do I...do I know you?" he asked.

"I should think so!" the young man said, smiling. "Good heavens, you have given me a scare! You sleep the sleep of the dead, if you don't mind my saying so."

"No, no, not at all," Snotty murmured, confused.

"It was hell waking you," the young man said. He laughed at Snotty's mistrustful look and, giving his shoulders an affectionate shake, said, "Snotty, it's Luc! Luc! Your old pal, remember?" He laughed again and led Snotty, unresisting, over to where a wing chair and a sky blue loveseat sat around a well appointed drinks tray.

"Luc," Snotty repeated vaguely as he sat down on the couch. "Oh yeah. I remember." Luc handed him a cigarette. As Snotty lit it, he noticed with surprise that the skin on his hands and arms was peeling. It wasn't painful, but it looked raw. Then he returned to grappling with the problem of Luc's identity. "I remember," he repeated. "I think."

Luc sat in the leather wing chair and deftly shook up a silver monogrammed cocktail shaker. From this he poured out two martinis into crystal glasses. "Luc," Snotty said, watching this with fascination. "Luc. Yeah. My friend." To his delight, his friend handed one of the glasses to him. To Snotty!

"You see, Snotty," Luc said in his bantering way. "One olive and one onion. Just the way you like it."

"Aw, Luc," Snotty said. "You remembered."

They clinked glasses.

"Chin chin," Luc said. And Snotty replied by lifting the thin crystal of his glass till it sparkled in the morning sun. Luc leaned back in his chair and gave a comfortable sigh. "This is what it's all about, isn't it, Snotty? Good times with good friends."

"You can say that again," Snotty agreed.

"After all," Luc said suavely, "you and I have so much in common—being both men of the world."

At this, Snotty paused. Just slightly. The glass, on the way to his lips, stopped for just a moment before continuing on. "Delicious, just delicious," he murmured. Then he remembered.[59]

"Yeah!" he said. "I remember now! My friend Luc! The Duke of New York!"

"Please, Snotty," Luc said, holding up a modest hand. "You know I don't like to use any of my titles among friends."

"Yeah, right, I got you, of course," Snotty said. He nodded a

---

59 Note the repeated motif of the problem of memory. This is the truly exciting motif of *Snotty Saves the Day*. If, as Arcadian scientists have discovered, fairy tales hold the laws of the physical universe, Snotty's repeated loss of memory would indicate why an entire society might suffer collective amnesia—as ours does.

vigorous agreement to the good taste his friend showed. "And I've always admired you for it. You know that."

"And you, Snotty," Luc said smoothly, topping off Snotty's glass. "What about you? You've always shown such reserve about your background. Why, I can't remember how many times you've stopped an admiring journalist from mentioning, in some magazine article or some Sunday supplement lifestyle piece, that your name means 'Of the House of Kings.'"

"Well, Luc, you know," Snotty said vaguely as Luc seemed to await a response. "It's not like we want everyone knowing our business, is it?"

"The hoi polloi," Luc agreed.

"Exactly," Snotty said. Sipping his drink, he noticed again that strange peeling of his skin. It left a layer much rosier and fresher looking than any he had ever noticed before.

"How well I remember your grandfather," Luc reminisced. "And how like him you are!"

"Good old grandpa," Snotty took a cautious puff on his cigarette.

"The Duke of Bulgaria!" Luc said. "Such a cultivated man! And your grandmother! The loveliest princess in Christendom. Of course, everyone was in love with her."

"But it was old grandpa that won her," Snotty chimed in, wiping a tear of pride from his eye.

"Exactly," Luc agreed. "At a grand tournament. He unseated three different knights!"

Snotty leaned forward in a confidential way. "Four," he said.

"Really?" Luc looked surprised. "I could have sworn.... But you would know, of course. Being his grandson and heir."

At this, Snotty spilled his drink on the sky blue couch. "Excuse me, Luc," he said, embarrassed. He tried to mop up the liquid with the tatters of his purple Teddy Bear clothes.

Then something stopped him. He suddenly saw it was beneath

him to clean up after himself, as if he were somebody unimportant, like a cleaning lady, or a schoolteacher. Instead, remembering his noble lineage, he held up the dregs in his glass for a toast.

"To Bulgaria!" he said.[60]

Luc, who had been watching this with an expression of satisfied pride, murmured, "Very good, Snotty. Noblesse oblige." Then he joined in the toast. "To Bulgaria," he agreed. And when Snotty looked down at himself, he saw, in some wonder, that he no longer wore the tattered plush of the Bears. He was dressed, instead, in leather and silk and expensive denim.

"Thanks, Luc," he said softly.

Luc just smiled and raised an eyebrow, as if to say that such trifles needn't be mentioned between friends. Instead, standing up, he gave himself a light tap on the forehead. "But here I am," he complained humorously, "forgetting all the rules of hospitality! Don't you think we should have a small bite to eat, before getting down to the business at hand?"

"Delighted," Snotty said with enthusiasm, and he, too, bounded to his feet, marveling as he did at the luxurious drape of his new clothes. He wondered privately how much they might have cost. He wondered what business Luc was talking about. But those thoughts disappeared the moment Snotty caught sight of what Luc considered 'a small bite to eat.' And Snotty was impressed. Truly, Luc had invited his friend Snotty to a royal feast.

---

60   Again, note how the character rewrites his history to suit his own needs. (See Bender Boyce-Flood, year 17.) Professor Grayling's notorious attempt to influence Arcadian literary tradition with the anonymous publication of the Siegfried Cycle is an example of this. (See Grayling, year 43.) In this work, which advertises itself as a pre-Amnesia epic of the Great Hero who led the Arcadian people out of the marshes into civilization in a Megalopolitan mold, there is a famous statement that the hero's descendants live on in the Grayling lineage! This work was exposed in masterful fashion by Dr. Fallaize in a series of trenchant articles written for *The Wrykyn Review* (year 58).

A banquet table as long as a stretch limousine stood there in the middle of the desert floor, the morning sunlight glinting off the heavy silver cutlery, the gold-rimmed china, the crystal goblets, and the white damask linens that covered it all. Not even the Gnomes' feast had come up to this. All the time that Snotty had run his business in Megalopolis, dodging threats and violence and arrest, he had always hoped, wistfully, in the back of his mind, that someone, somewhere, would see what he was doing and admire and appreciate it. And that people would show that admiration and appreciation by giving parties in his honor. Parties just like this.

It was a fine feast. There was a whole ham, its brown glazed fat studded with cloves. There were white asparagus as thick as Snotty's wrist, dripping with butter. There was a pyramid of red candy apples. And an enormous platter piled high with the fattest, most golden, oiliest chips Snotty had ever seen, all toothsome and savory. Next to them was a crystal cruet of walnut-colored vinegar.

"Not that I eat like this just any day," Luc joked. "Only when I have a guest I admire and appreciate and want to impress."

At this, tears leapt to Snotty's eyes. But he turned his head and wiped them quickly away before Luc could see. Filled with confidence now, Snotty picked up one of the huge, gold-rimmed plates and piled it high with helpings of chips and thick slices of steaming hot ham. "This is great, Luc, really," Snotty said as he gave the crispy chips a couple of hefty shakes from the vinegar cruet. "Thanks a lot."

"No nettle greens there, eh?" Luc said in a casual tone.

Snotty paused at this and blinked, as if some vague memory had passed through his head. A griping pain in the lower part of his gut was making itself known more insistently than before. He thought now that he'd felt this pain from the minute he'd woken on the desert floor. It was a nagging tightness in his belly, and it seemed to be getting worse.

Hunger pangs, Snotty decided. He couldn't think what else it could be. He was hungry. But when he looked at the food piled high on his plate, his face, in spite of himself, settled into an expression of faint disgust.

Uncertain, Snotty looked at Luc and tried to smile. He saw the beautiful young man watch him closely from under hooded eyes. Snotty knew, all of a sudden, that Luc didn't want him to know how closely he watched.

This put Snotty on his guard—but against what, he didn't know. Automatically he took up a fork and began to eat. He chewed his way dutifully through a half a plate of food until, fretful, he pushed his plate away.

"Nothing wrong, I hope?" Luc said in his smooth way. "Nothing to intrude a false note?"

Snotty rubbed at his forehead and noticed that his skin was peeling off his face, as well as off his hands and arms. Lifting his shirt, he saw the same thing happening on his stomach. He could feel the skin peeling on his back, too.

Luc cleared his throat.

"Sorry, Luc," Snotty said, ashamed, because for a minute there he had forgotten Luc was there at all. He felt rude and vulgar and embarrassed.

Luc, ever tactful, ignored this. Instead, he knit his eyebrows together and brought his long white fingers into a tapping, meditating steeple.

"Speak to me, Snotty," he urged finally in the gentlest of voices. "There should be no secrets between business partners."

"Business partners?" Snotty said, astonished. He looked at Luc to see if he was making fun of him. "Are we business partners?"

"Of course we're business partners," Luc said smoothly, and passed Snotty a platter loaded with chocolate and whipped cream cakes. "Don't you remember? You work for me," he prompted. "You're the best. The star of the organization. My most up-and-coming boy."

"The star of the organization," Snotty repeated, scratching at his stomach. The new skin left behind by the peeling of the old itched under his new clothes. Snotty was surprised to realize he missed his old, worn-in Teddy Bear outfit. And the cramping in his stomach got worse. He took a bite of the ham and chips, but they had cooled down now, and they tasted dusty and old and mean. "Yeah," he said in an automatic voice. "Yeah, I think I remember."

"Have a cake," Luc advised in his calm way.

"I will," Snotty agreed. "Thanks." But even as he bit into the luscious filling between slices of sponge light as air, he couldn't stop a stricken look that crept onto his face.

"You were the star of the organization," Luc continued, as if he hadn't noticed any of this. "And so I made you—you, and you only—a full partner in the business."

At this Snotty gave Luc a quick look, one that was both deeper and more earnest than any he had given before.

"Out of admiration and appreciation for your hard work and brilliance," Luc said warmly. "You deserve it, Snotty. You really do."

"Sure," Snotty agreed in an unhappy voice. "Thanks."

"With this promotion," Luc went on, "your days of proving yourself are over. Now others can prove themselves to you. You're at the top. The pinnacle of your profession. The peak."

"The peak," Snotty repeated vaguely. "The Peak of Transcendence. I remember."

"Yes," Luc said, pleased. "The Peak of Transcendence, indeed."[61]

The two were silent. Snotty, made uneasy by this, reached for a candy apple. But it tasted sickeningly sweet, and the apple under the flabby sugar coating was mealy and didn't have much flavor. So he put it aside.

"Only one person at a time can sit on top of the Peak," Luc

---

61 Curiously enough, the Neofundamentalist forces have chosen the image of such a peak for their insignia: a shining snow-covered silver mountain on a field of azure.

reminded Snotty, watching him.

"Yeah," Snotty said. And then there was silence again.

Luc moved restlessly in his chair. Snotty could see that Luc didn't like silence either. The beautiful young man snapped his fingers, and a military band—complete with bagpipes—appeared and began to play.

"Ah," Luc said, settling back into his chair. "That's better."

But Snotty didn't think it was better after all. Confused, he squirmed on his spindly gold seat.

"Yes, Snotty," Luc continued. "You're a full partner now. That's the meaning of Success. You're the Biggest. The Best. Everyone looks up to you. Everyone fears you. Everyone envies you. This is what I have done for you."

This seemed to call for an answer. "Thanks," Snotty finally said, though he couldn't help but feel it was a lame response.

If it was lame, Luc either didn't notice or decided, for reasons of his own, to overlook it. His eloquence was in full flood now, and he ran his perfect fingers through his glossy black hair in his excitement. "And you deserve it, Snotty!" he said. "You do! You, who were the lowest of the low in your world, you of all people understand that there must be Those Who Rule and Those Who Are Ruled. THAT is the True Law of Everywhere. You of all people understand that the Universal Destiny is Big and Grand, not Small and Humble. That it is Strong and Powerful, not Foolish and Weak!" Luc's face clouded and grew ugly with anger. "Others," he said briefly, "have not understood this so well as you."[62]

"The Teddy Bears," Snotty said before he knew what he was saying. Then he looked confused. Who or what were the Teddy Bears? He couldn't remember. All he knew was that, whatever they were, they were against Luc.

---

62   Professor Grayling insists this scene is a later corruption of the original text, which must have meant the words of Luc to be the words of Wisdom. In this, he is profoundly mistaken.

"Among others," Luc said. His eyes flashed.

A sudden panic gripped Snotty. He had lost something! Shoving his maimed hand first into one pocket of his new clothes, then into the other, he knew he missed it. But what was it?

"They refused to acknowledge those put in authority above them," Luc said.

"That's bad," Snotty said, although he was only half paying attention. In shoving his hand into his pockets, he had torn open his wound. Its throbbing distracted him. He looked at his little finger's stump and saw it start to bleed again.

That was when he remembered. The Key. He had lost the Rose Gold Key!

"Miserable bits of fluff!" Luc said contemptuously. "Toys, not men! They were never worthy to have you among them!"

"Me among them," Snotty murmured. Where was the Key? He couldn't remember. He could only remember that it was important. His Teddy Bear clothes. The Key had been in his Teddy Bear clothes. But what were they? Where were they? Covertly, Snotty began to scan the desert floor.

"You!" Luc continued. "You, Snotty the Great! Snotty of the House of Kings! Snotty the SUN GOD!"

At this, Snotty looked at Luc. His jaw opened and shut. "I do know you," he said finally. "I do." And, once more, he forgot the Key.

Luc stared deeply into Snotty's eyes and put his hands on him, one on each shoulder. "From the earliest age, Snotty, you understood. You understood completely that the Strong rule the Weak. And that for the Big to possess the World is the only Law. To make sure nothing is left that is miserable, crawling, mean, or small."

"I know who you are!" Snotty said. "You're Mr. Big!"

The moment he said it, he knew it was right. Luc was many things. But among them, he was Mr. Big.

Chapter XX

SNOTTY'S CHOICE

Luc was much moved.

"You know me, then," he said, and his gaze deepened.

"Yes," Snotty said after a moment. "I do know you. I think I've known you a long time."

At this, Snotty got up awkwardly from his seat and shifted from foot to foot in the sand.

"I've been working for you, haven't I?" he said quietly. "I pretended I made you up, but I knew that wasn't true. I always knew you were real."

"You were a smart boy," Luc agreed. "One of my favorites. And you never cried."

"No." Snotty gave an unhappy smile at this mention of his accomplishments. "You've been with me all along, haven't you, Luc? Ever since I can remember. And with my mother. And with everyone on Hamercy Street, too."

Snotty could remember his home now. But the memory was a mean and shabby one. There was no pleasure in it.

"They never could see me," Luc said in a tender voice. "They never had the vision. They never had the nerve. Not like you."

Snotty looked away. "What do you mean?" he said shyly, kicking at the sand.

Then something down there caught his eye. A glint of gold. And there it was: the Key. It lay there, under a dusting of sand, shining in the sun.

Luc didn't see it. He was too busy scanning the horizon. Quickly,

Snotty scooped up the Key.

Luc seemed to make a decision. Draping one arm around Snotty's shoulders, he wheeled him around and walked them both out briskly onto the desert.

"I mean, Snotty," he said, "something you already know. It's lonely at the top."

Snotty nodded. He had found this himself, both in his career in Megalopolis and in his brief reign as the Sun God.

"Yes," he agreed.

"When I find someone I can talk to—really talk to—I like to keep them close. I like to reward them for being my friend."

"You want to be my friend," Snotty said. He hefted the Key in his pocket, folding his fingers around it to keep it safe.

"In a word," Luc confirmed expansively. "And in exchange...look!"

Luc swept an arm in front of them, toward the vista ahead.

Snotty's eyes focused, then widened. "Wow," he said simply. And he ran toward the marvelous sight.

———————

A plateau had appeared on the desert: a shelf, a butte, jutting out over the expanse of dead sand. On it was a telescope: big, old-fashioned, heavy, made of greenish bronze, trimmed with an ornamental footplate and a coin slot to make it work. This pointed over the desert plain, which was covered by a morning fog behind which the Mountains of Resistance had disappeared. A mist rising from this fog crept up the sides of the Peak of Transcendence. And when the fog parted, at the foot of the Peak, Snotty saw the great city of Megalopolis!

"Wow!" he said again as he reached the plateau.

There it was, Megalopolis: mighty, vast, humming and buzzing, writhing on the desert floor. And looming over it, as pure, unattainable, and desirable as ever, the Peak of Transcendence glistened in the noonday sun.

Snotty sucked in his breath in wonder and touched the enormous telescope with a doubtful hand.

"Allow me," Luc said smoothly behind him. Luc's beautiful slim hand snaked around his neck and put a silver coin in the telescope's slot.

"WOW!" Snotty yelled, his breath rushing out. He jumped on the telescope's wrought iron step and peered through the eyepiece at the city below. "I can see my house!" Just then the telescope clicked shut. Snotty groaned with disappointment. But Luc produced more coins from his perfectly tailored pockets and poured them into the slot. And so Snotty could swing the telescope first this way, then that, exclaiming at the sights.

"Look! I can see the docks at Mega Harbor! And the phone mast in the schoolyard! There's the police station! Incredible!"

There they were, all the scenes from his life. And not just his life, but the dreams he had for his life, as well. There were the glittering boulevards choked with traffic! There were the shops bulging with expensive goods! There were the grand buildings!

"Tilt up the lens," Luc urged. He put a large gold coin in the slot and pushed at the telescope gently.

Snotty, obedient, looked. And there, over Megalopolis, loomed the Peak of Transcendence. And Snotty saw for the first time that what fueled the great city was desire for the Peak.

He could see everyone in Megalopolis. They climbed over each other to get to the top of the Peak. And the energy they generated, squabbling and clawing, was the fuel that powered the giant city. He, Snotty, had been the fuel that powered Megalopolis. He and everyone in it.[63]

---

63 Here we see hints of the founding legend of Arcadia: rejection of the slavery of power in exchange for the freedom of equity. A perfect example of how the story can be

Luc studied him carefully now. Intent on a line of thought, his hand fell away from the telescope. He didn't notice when the mirage of Megalopolis began to dissolve.

"Then we'll finish up the formalities, shall we?" he said in a brisk tone. "The contract and so on. Our partnership agreement. All that's customary in these cases. I'm sure you want to do everything right."

"Oh yeah," Snotty said, looking at him unhappily. "Sure." As Luc patted his pockets for a pen, Snotty darted up for one last look.

Recognizing his mistake, Luc shot out a hand to block Snotty's view. But Snotty was too quick. As Snotty squinted through the eyepiece, the great city of Megalopolis began to disappear, rolling up like a piece of painted canvas. Behind it, the desert revealed itself. And poking up from a mound of sand was the broken paw of a Teddy Bear.

At this, the gold coin's credit ran out. The black shade of the eyepiece clicked shut. On the platform, Snotty stepped back from the telescope.

"Something the matter?" Luc said in his calm way. But he watched the boy with a veiled look.

"What?" Snotty said vaguely. He shook himself, as if he were cold. "No," he said finally. "Nothing's the matter."

"You seem disturbed," Luc said, probing delicately, hiding his impatience.

"I'm not..."

"Distracted..."

At this, Snotty wheeled around and bawled, "Just leave me alone, okay?" He turned and walked into the desert alone.

Luc, apparently untroubled, brought his fine fingers together again in their tapping, meditative steeple. He waited, composed, until

---

a foundation of culture. (See Bender Boyce-Flood, year 17.) In fact, so perfect is it that I begin to suspect the story of Snotty is not just legend. But this is a radical analysis, requiring more thought.

Snotty, not knowing what else to do, wandered back.

"That's your city then," Snotty said finally.

"One of them," Luc conceded. "Yes."

Snotty nodded as if this only confirmed what he knew already.

"It can be your city, too," Luc reminded him.

"I know," Snotty said dully. Luc frowned.

Luc waited patiently while Snotty kicked up sand with his toe. But there were indications that this patience was wearing thin. "Look at me, Snotty," Luc said sharply. When Snotty didn't, but instead turned and walked away, shoulders hunched and hands in his pockets, Luc's expression changed.

"I've offered to be your friend," Luc called after him warningly.

Snotty looked back at him, troubled. "Yeah," he said. "You did that before. When I was a little kid."

"That's right," Luc said, and the tenderness returned to his voice. "I'm pleased you remember." When Snotty stayed silent, he said, "From the first, you were one of my favorite boys."

Snotty muttered something under his breath.

"What?" Luc said sharply. "I can't hear you."

Snotty mumbled just loud enough to be understood. "I said I wasn't a boy then, not when you and I first met. I was a girl."

This was the truth. Snotty had been born a girl, and her mother had named her Lily. But there was only one thing lower, in Megalopolis, than a poor little boy from Widdleshift, in the neighborhood of Makewater, in the district of Hackendosh, part of the ancient county of Queerspittle, in the northwest of East New York. Only one thing was more scorned in Megalopolis than a poor little boy. And that was a poor little girl. It hadn't taken Lily long to understand this, and when she did, she turned herself into Snotty. Her mother didn't care. By and by, Lily was forgotten. It was easier that way, all round.[64]

---

64   A startling turn of events in the story, which foretells startling turns in the culture. See Arcadian history and its rejection of the imperial protection of Megalopolis in favor

But Snotty, try as he might, hadn't forgotten. He tried, but he just couldn't do it. He remembered how Luc had helped him become Snotty, helped him every step of the way. Had helped her. Snotty remembered now that she was Lily, and, as Lily, she forced herself to look Luc in the eye. "I'm not a boy, all right?" she said, all fierce. "I'm a girl. Okay?"

"Oh," Luc said, relaxing into a chair that appeared next to him. "Of course I know that. Who better?" Another chair appeared. He indicated Snotty should sit down.

But Snotty didn't. "I know you know," she said, troubled, looking at Luc. "But why didn't you let on?"

"Honestly, Snotty," Luc said with an irritable wave of his hand. "It's old news. You were a girl; you wanted to be a boy. What's wrong with that? Desires like that power the whole world. If everyone were happy to be who they are, where would we be? Nowhere. Megalopolis? A village. I wouldn't be interested in it, anyway." Propping his elbows on his knees and cupping his chin in his hand, Luc looked at Snotty. "You wanted to be a boy. I helped you pretend. Now I can do more."

"You can do more," Snotty said. Her dark brown eyes had an odd and distant look. "I know you can do more than that," she said. And strange as it was, she did know.

"Exactly," Luc said. "I can make you a real boy."

Snotty repeated, "You can make me a real boy."

"I can do so much more than that," Luc said. In the silence that followed, Snotty knew this was true.

"It's why you've come here," Luc went on, his voice soft and low. "And how you found me. The force of your desire."

A troubled Snotty turned away. Was it true? Was that the whole secret of her adventure? Or was there something else?

"There is something else," she thought. "I know there is. But

---

of a more homely magistrate culture, years 1 to 3, before the ascension of Queen Lily the Silent.

what? I wish I could remember." In her pocket, she closed her hand around the Key.

"I can make you a real boy, Snotty," Luc repeated, watching her. "Then you'll grow into a man. And what a man! Respected, feared, envied by all. With me beside you, you'll rule over your fellows. Your word will be law; your anger, death. You'll be as good as a god." Luc's expression softened with pride. "I've watched you, Snotty," he said. "Many's the time I've said to myself, 'This is my boy, and I must say I am well pleased.' " He smiled. "Snotty," he said softly. "Snotty the Sun God."

Snotty's hand gripped the Key.

"Why me?" she said.

"What?" Luc said, startled.

"I mean," Snotty said, her expression intent as she tried to understand, "there's got to be some reason. Something in it for you. You offering me all this. Why ME?"

Luc laughed his beautiful laugh. "You always were a shrewd one, Snotty," he said. He leaned forward, looking Snotty in the eye, his turquoise eyes shining. "Think of what it would mean to you. Wealth. Power. Your dreams come true."

But Snotty, being shrewd, saw right away that he hadn't answered her question. This made her think.

"I helped you pretend to be a boy," Luc said. "Now I have the power to turn you into one for real." He stood up and came over beside her.

Snotty looked up at Luc. She clutched the Key. She held her breath. And she said, "What if I don't want to anymore?"

She braced herself, waiting for Luc's rage. But instead, he laughed again and said, "Oh, Snotty! I understand you better than you understand yourself." With an ironic half-bow, he said, "Look and see." And his hand swept out in a gesture out over the plain.

Snotty looked. There was nothing but gold sand.

Luc put an amused finger beside his nose. "Wait," he said.

The wind rose up. Luc controlled it, Snotty saw, moving his right hand up and down like a conductor bringing his orchestra to order. And the wind blew. The wind blew hard.

The wind blew harder and harder and harder. Snotty tried, but found that she couldn't stand up against it. She fell down into the sand, choking and sputtering, the same as she had done the night before, the night she had now forgotten.

The night before. Its hidden memory just showed itself, as if, buried under the sand, the wind now uncovered it. Just as the wind now uncovered what was buried under the desert floor.

"Look," Luc said in a soft voice, as the wind died away. He helped Snotty to her feet. Brushing herself off, she looked.

The wind had blown the loose sand off the desert, revealing the site of the Teddy Bear massacre beneath.

"Wha...wha...wha...," Snotty gasped. She backed up, her breath coming hard. Then she wheeled about and shrieked at Luc. "WHAT HAVE YOU DONE?" And screaming, "Big Teddy! Snowflake! Melia! Tuxton!" she ran out into the midst of the ghastly remains.

Snotty ran on, squeaking, sounds fighting to come out of her little body. These choked and disappeared as soon as they got to the air. She ran, recognizing in the torn, burnt bits of porcelain and plush the companions of her days in the Mountains of Resistance, of the days when she remembered who she really was, of the days when she remembered she was a girl after all.

Those jagged, shattered bits of china—who were they?

And that garroted plush bag?

The mutilated Tuxton, the white stuffing where his muzzle had been now a corrupt gray.

The half-burnt corpse of the Dog.

Snotty ran among these horrors, back and forth, forth and back, squeaking like a bat, waving her arms in an ungainly way that made

Luc laugh out loud.

"Very amusing, my dear," he called out. "Though not exactly worthy of a Sun God."

Shudders wracked Snotty's frame. The only thing alive in that desert was her own small self. And Luc.

Then she saw, sticking up from a bit of burnt cloth and sand, one half of a mangled head.

Snotty gave a frightened choke and sank down beside it. What she had feared was true. This—this torn and distorted bit of toy—was all that was left of Big Teddy.

She picked at the bit of dirty plush, as if afraid of what it might do. Then she pulled it close to her narrow little chest, cradling it there. As she did, her biggest fear, the fear that had followed her from as far back as she could remember, got bigger and bigger and bigger until she couldn't hold it anymore. But she refused to give in. She wouldn't cry.

"Quite right," Luc said, approving. Walking over to Snotty, he crouched down beside her and looked at her with a sympathetic eye. "You're right not to cry." He looked around the battlefield now with the eye of a connoisseur. "This won't be the last battle you'll see. And it will always be the same. The Strong will always beat the Weak. Always. You've done the right thing, choosing the side of the Strong."

Snotty, mouth gaping, looked at him, then looked away. She knew what he was saying. "Choose me, Snotty, or be like THEM." Like them—the torn bits of fluff, blown by the wind, unburied, forgotten.

"I can bury Big Teddy," she thought, even though she couldn't, not really—the noble Bear was too thoroughly torn apart. "I can do that." I don't know where she learnt to do this, because in Megalopolis the dead were taken away in vans and never seen again. But somehow she knew. Without answering Luc, she dug there in front of her in the desert sand.

As she scrabbled there, tearing at the ground with her fingernails, some liquid bubbled up from the sand. As she dug deeper and deeper, the small bubbling became a small pool. And then a small spring.

Snotty, without knowing it, had uncovered one of the many springs of the Stream of the Mountains, which ran hidden under the Plains on its way to the Sea.

She was thirsty. So she scooped up some of the spring's water, and drank it down.

And then she did something she had never done in her short life. She began to cry.

Snotty cried. She cried and cried. Sobs poured out of her. Her face twisted and quivered, and her nose ran with snot. She choked. She gagged.

And still Lily cried.[65]

---

65   Commonly believed by scholars to be an allegorical depiction of the conflict between Megalopolis and Arcadia. But Sivia disputes this thesis, theorizing that allegory indicates actual history. (See Sivia, year 59. Also see Fallaize, year 61, chapter seven, "Allegory or Reality?") And my own belief begins to take me further.

Chapter XXI

LILY AND LUC

Days and weeks passed, then months and years. As Lily cried, every kind of weather pummeled the Plains: sun, rain, wind, snow. From hot to windy to cold to wet and back to hot again. But no matter how many seasons passed overhead, Lily stayed the age she was, which was twelve going on thirteen.[66]

Her skin kept peeling. The top layer rubbed right off and left behind skin that was pink and raw. Twenty years passed, then thirty. Lily's new skin smoothed out, losing its rough look. It turned a rosy olive gold under a sheen of smooth brown. Her black hair grew and curled around her ears. Her face changed.

Fifty years passed. Sixty years. Seventy. Then, after a hundred years, another change.

After a hundred years of crying, Lily had shed so many tears in one spot—the spot where the Stream bubbled up through the dead sand—that rivulets of water from the spring mixed with her tears, cutting tiny streams in the desert. Here and there the streams dammed up against some obstacle, making first puddles, and then ponds. Lily found herself beside one of these. It was in its reflection that she saw for the first time the change in her own looks.

Surprised, she felt her tears cool. Now they came in steady warm

---

66   Once thought impossible, but Arcadian physics has proved that Time may stop while Historical and Personal Transformation occurs. (See Sivia, year 59.) There can be no greater historical or personal transformation in Arcadian history than that of Snotty into Lily. And, if I am right—if Snotty is actually Lily, our first queen—this transformation changed our landscape, our culture, our world at the same time.

droplets that made a firm plop as they fell onto the sand.

After awhile—maybe twenty or thirty years—a green sprout appeared in the spot where her tears fell. This grew fast (maybe another twenty-five years) into a sturdy tree with a wide crown of pale and dark green leaves.

Lily's tears slowed now.

Then there came among the leaves of the tree many white and pink buds. Blossoming, they scented the air. Lily's nose twitched with pleasure. As she smiled (the first time in two centuries that she had), she watched the blossoms become apples: first tiny and gold, then larger and red and pink and green. These ripened in the sun that crept up over the Plains.

Time slowed. The sun paused. Grateful for this, Lily tilted her head to feel its warmth on her face. Tired after her hundred years of grief, she closed her eyes.

Now she heard a tap, tap, tap coming toward her, as two pairs of dainty hooves picked their way across the rivulets of water. Lily opened her eyes and saw Snowflake.

His eyes were clear. His coat was white. His hooves were silver. And in between his emerald eyes was a white and silver horn.

"Snowflake," Lily said. But the minute she said it, she knew it was wrong. Snowflake was no more this horse's true name than Snotty was hers. It was the name of some part of the little horse that extended into this time and place. He had many names. Lily saw that now. She realized that this must be true of her, as well.[67]

"I don't know what to call you," Lily said. Snowflake just smiled at this, and, kneeling in front of her, lowered himself to the ground. Careful of his white and silver horn, he laid his head in Lily's lap.

"Snowflake," she said again, not meaning to be insulting in reminding him of a name that wasn't all he was, and that meant all

---

67   The Law of Many Realities is a known fact. I have often remarked that where it is in dispute, there political, rather than scientific, forces are at work. A bitter truth.

And in between his emerald eyes was a single white and silver horn.

sorts of pains and humiliations, perhaps the worst of which she had been responsible for. But she used that name because it was the name that meant the connection between them in that web she saw at the top of the trees. As she petted the unicorn on his velvet muzzle, she saw, in the desert in front of her, that same web. It had been there all along without her being able to see. She could see it now. And she could see each thread between each point in the web. At each point was one of her dead friends. All the corpses that had long since decayed into the sand over her hundreds of years of tears had come back to life. She could see them all: Tuxton, and Melia, and the Dog. There they were, all the Bears, gathered around the apple tree, peering at her with a benevolence that she had seen many times before, but never, before now, recognized for what it was. The Bears smiled and nodded, and even Tuxton's restored muzzle was so real she was sure she could reach out and touch it. This impression was so strong that she did lift one hand—the hand with the maimed finger—and saw that it held the Key. And the Bears and the Dog in front of her were real, as real as she. They shook themselves off, laughing and talking among themselves as if sharing what had gone on with them all those hundreds of years they had lain, in defeat and death, decaying under the desert floor.

"Tuxton!" Lily whispered. "Melia! Dog! Is this really you?" The creatures smiled at her in silence. They hadn't come close enough to her to be heard yet, although she could hear faint snatches of their conversations among themselves. Somehow she knew, though, that they had returned. Somehow they had returned to her from defeat and death.

The Dog nuzzled Lily under her arm, tossing her elbow up and away from her face. Lily looped her arm around the Dog's neck as he licked her cheek.

Lily closed her eyes. When she opened them, she saw her friends were now completely real. They rushed up to greet her, all the Bears, and Creatures, and Pleasures, and there was a clamor of excited reunions. Hundreds of paws wrung Lily's hand.

"But where's Big Teddy?" she asked as Fion and Mion thumped her on the back, and Tia turned a cartwheel.

At this, the clamor died, and the Toys hung their heads. The Dog gave a low growl, looking at Tuxton Ted. The silly-looking Bear stepped forward. Lily rejoiced to see his face miraculously restored. He hesitated before he spoke.

"They tore her into too many pieces, Snotty," he said in his worried voice. "She can never come back."

All were silent now. A mournful wind whistled past. After awhile, Lily said, "I'm not Snotty, Tuxton. My name is Lily."

Tuxton smiled. "Why, Lily," he said. "We all knew that." As the silly-looking Bear spoke, Lily saw the shape of his face flicker and shift. For a second, she thought she saw something that wasn't silly—something that wasn't even a Teddy Bear at all. Then it was gone.[68]

"Tuxton," Lily said, meaning to ask him about this. Was Tuxton even his real name? Or was it, like Snowflake's, only part of a much larger whole?

She never got to ask him, though. She had forgotten Luc. And, of course, if there were more to Tuxton than met the eye, and more to Snowflake, and more to Lily herself, how much more would there be to him?

---

68   "To be moved by a child's story is to be moved by our own history." Sophia the Wise. Our second queen was often heard to repeat this maxim, especially to children. Did she suspect? Or did she know the truth all along?

Chapter XXII

SNOTTY SAVES THE DAY

Suddenly there was a white rush of sound, a roar. The Bears, and the Dog, and the Unicorn, and all the other Creatures leapt up as one. They were frightened. But they were together, and they held their ground.

A colossus stood astride the horizon: a fire-breathing giant. Its head, on monstrous shoulders, was lost in the clouds. Its hands, big as mountains, grabbed two of the clouds floating across its neck and banged them hard, one into the other.

"CCCRRRAAAACCCCKKKK!!!" thundered the clouds, and a lightning bolt shot out from between them, dashing to the ground at Snowflake's feet. The unicorn whinnied and rose up on his hind legs.

"I AM SERIOUSLY DISPLEASED!" bellowed the Monster, his breath shooting out smoke and brimstone, and the booming timbre of his voice forcing them all to clap paws and hands over ears. "WE WILL MASSACRE YOU ALL OVER AGAIN!"

At this, the Gnome Army loomed again, massive and powerful as before, on all sides. Lily and the Teddy Bear Army were surrounded.

Lily looked at her companions. The Teddy Bears were afraid—how could they help it?—but they showed a determination to do what they had always done through Time. They would do what they had to. The Toys drew themselves up, ready.

The clouds around the Monstrous Giant's head cleared away. Lily saw the Monster was Luc.

This made her mad.

"FIGHT ME, SNOTTY!" the huge, fire-breathing Monster called

out from above. "IF YOU DARE!"

At this, something dark and painful stirred in Lily. She was angry. And it seemed to her she was no longer Lily. She was Snotty. Snotty the Sun God.

"If I DARE?" Snotty said, in a fury. She didn't pay attention when Tuxton placed a warning paw on her arm. She shook him off instead.

"I am SNOTTY!" Snotty bellowed. "Snotty the SUN GOD! I will fight and fight and go on fighting until there's nothing left of me and my friends!"

Lily would have asked her friends what they thought of this plan. But Snotty, in his fury, forgot. A Sun God, as we all know, never asks a mere mortal for advice.[69]

Also Snotty was in a rage. All this made him forget everything he had learned up till that moment. Now he rushed at Luc's legs, which had grown bigger than tree stumps, and pounded at them with his tiny fists.

"HAH!" breathed Luc above him. There was a note of triumph in the echo of his voice.

Tuxton bowed his head. Snowflake gave a distressed whinny. And Lily, hidden somewhere in the angry Snotty, heard.

So Snotty stopped. And the moment he stopped, everything else stopped, too.

It was as if everything—the Gnomes, the Teddy Bear Army, even the landscape and the weather—waited for him to decide.

But decide what?

Snotty turned, restless and angry, back to Tuxton. "What's the GOOD of it?" he said. But Tuxton didn't speak.

Snotty turned to Snowflake. "What's the point to being small and weak, and on the losing side?" But Snowflake didn't answer. He pawed the ground, his emerald eyes hidden behind their long silver

---

69   An amusing note: a common Arcadian folk saying has it that this is the difference between our own country and Megalopolis.

lashes.

Snotty turned to Tia, Fia, Fion, Mion, Melia and Lui. "What's the use of having friends, or of being happy, if these things make you weak? What's the use if it's always the same fight, and always a fight against forces so Strong that you can never, ever hope to win? What's the use of it?"[70]

But Tia, Fia, Fion, Mion, Melia and Lui didn't answer. They looked down at the ground, their paws folded in front of them.

"The Weak always lose," a suave voice said in Snotty's ear. It was Luc. He stood there, elegant as before, his old self, Snotty's friend. "The Strong always Win."

Snotty knew this was true. His past life in Megalopolis had shown exactly that. Nothing in Snotty's life had ever shown him that the Weak, or the Unimportant (which came to the same thing), were worth anything at all.

All his life he, Snotty, had worked to be Strong. He had worked hard. He had proved himself stronger and more important than the other boys and than all the villains of his world. He, Snotty, was stronger than them all! He was Snotty the Sun God! He would never be weak again! To be Weak was to be Small, and to be Small in Megalopolis was the lowest thing of all.

"Father of Lies," a soft voice said. "Father of Lies from the beginning." It was Tuxton. Snotty saw a stern look on his plush face.

"I beg your pardon?" said Luc, plainly startled. He recovered his poise right away. "Snotty," he said in a haughty tone—the kind of voice that Snotty had once admired and tried to imitate—"Snotty, perhaps you'd introduce me to your friends."

Snowflake stepped up beside Tuxton and pawed at the ground with one silver hoof. "There have been times," Snowflake said gravely,

---

70   The very argument recently used to advance a cowardly strategy of surrender to the Neofundamentalist forces and their Megalopolitan masters. A strategy rightly to be despised.

"when the Weak have conquered the Strong, oh, Prince! There have been many such times."

"Excuse me," Luc said. It was obvious he was very angry indeed. "Do I KNOW you?"

Tia, Fia, Fion, Mion, Melia and Lui came forward now, and Melia spoke for them all in a clear, high voice. "You know us, Son of the Morning. You have fought us many times. Many times have we fought and many times have we won. But we disdained to trumpet our Triumph, resting instead with Truth."

Luc looked at them with disgust. "What gibberish," he complained. "What vulgarity. How very unscientific, too. Honestly, where do they get this kind of thing? And in the modern world. It's a scandal." He gave a fastidious flick of the fingers to a bit of fluff on his elegant clothes. "This kind of thing won't be allowed when you and I are in charge, eh, Snotty?"

Snotty, who had been watching Tuxton and Snowflake and the Girl Bears, turned back to Luc now. "About that being in charge, Luc," he said. "What does that mean? Exactly?"[71]

Luc, his good humor now restored, draped his arm around Snotty's shoulders as the two walked past the saluting Gnomes. "Well, Snotty, of course it means being at the top, and making sure everyone underneath does exactly what they're told."

"And when there are rebellions, we put them down," Snotty said.

"Of course," Luc said. "It's our duty."

"Then we tell the rebels—the Weak—what to do."

"Absolutely. It's amazing how little the Weak understand of what is truly good for them."

"So would you say then," Snotty continued in a casual way, "that we need the Weak—the ones at the bottom—more than they need us?"

Luc stopped and stared. "What do you mean?"

---

71 Another Arcadian folk saying: "Being in charge? What does that mean?" Often quoted by Lily the Silent.

"I mean, if we're going to be conquerors...if we're going to be on the top...doesn't there have to be something to be conquered? Somebody? Doesn't there have to be somebody on the bottom? If we're the Strong, don't we need to have the Weak?"

"Of course," Luc said, an icy glint in his eye.

"So we have to have them. We need the Weak. But it seems to me, Luc, that the Weak don't need us. If the Weak disappear, then so do we, the Strong," he went on to explain. "But if the Strong disappear, well, then, the Weak can just go back to minding their own business. They can get on with things. Which means," he said thoughtfully, "that the Weak are stronger than the Strong. If you get my meaning."[72]

Luc looked at him haughtily. "No I don't," he said in an ice-cold voice. "It seems to me you've missed the main point. The Weak want to conquer US."

"Do they, Luc?" Snotty asked.

"Doesn't everyone, Snotty?" Luc said. He raked the Teddy Bear Army with a look of disdain.

"No," Snotty said almost with regret. He remembered what it was like in the Mountains, in the Teddy Bear Camp. "No, I don't think everybody does want to conquer what there is to be conquered." He took a deep, deep breath.

"I don't want to, myself," he said. "It's just a great big waste of time. I don't want to be Snotty the Sun God—not anymore. I just want to be...myself."

As Snotty said this, he changed into Lily once and for all. Snotty gave up being the Sun God for good. This took nerve. But Snotty was, always, a brave boy.

---

72   This is, of course, a long-standing political debate in our world. And THE cause of our present war.

That was the end of Snotty the Sun God's story.

––––––––––

But it was the beginning of Lily's.[73]

––––––––––

At this, a shout went up from among the Gnomes.

"Look!" the Large Gnome cried.

"Stop them!" the Medium Gnome bawled.

"Oh, NO!" the Small Gnome squealed.

All across the desert, the Teddy Bear Army turned, one by one, into a bunch of lifeless Toys.

"NOOOO!" the Small Gnome squeaked again, running among them, giving one a buffet here, and kicking another one there, as if to get them to turn back. But none of the Toys did more, now, than fall on their sides and lie there. They couldn't stand upright on their own, much less fight.

The Gnome Army was now in disarray. The discipline of the troops disappeared, evaporating in their terror at the nonexistence of the enemy. Panic spread. Gnome Soldiers fled in all directions.

Snowflake became a pretty little rocking horse, and the Dog pranced about wanting to play as the Gnomes ran over each other in their hurry to retreat.

"Snotty!" Luc shouted over the melee. "Rally the troops!" To the fleeing Gnomes, he shouted, "Your Sun God commands you! Stop!"

---

73 Note the connection between the beginning of a story and an actual birth first made by Prof. Grayling. (See Grayling, year 41.) The point was made only in passing, but I believe it to be important. Note also that no birth records exist in Arcadia before year 1. Another indication that *Snotty Saves the Day* portrays the birth not just of an individual, but of Arcadia as well.

But there was no more Sun God. And Lily stayed where she was.

"Snotty!" Luc said angrily. "Remember who you are!"

"Oh yes," Lily said. "I do."

"Then order them to stop!"

Lily looked at Luc, then turned back to where the stuffed animals lay tumbled about in the desert sun. "I don't think they would listen to me," she said briefly, and then she went to a stuffed Tuxton, who had fallen on his snout in the sand. Bending over the silly looking stuffed Bear, Lily wiped the dirt off his muzzle and sat him upright.

Meanwhile, the Gnome Army disappeared. Only Luc and Lily were left. Luc stood there, staring with chagrin at the horizon over which his departing Army had fled. Lily ignored him.

"Very good, girl," he said after a moment's reflection. He brought his hands together in ironical applause. "Excellent strategy. Hide your strength and live to fight another day! Allow me to congratulate you."

"Thanks," Lily said shortly. She continued seating Tia, Fia, Fion, Mion, Melia and Lui in a lopsided cluster. Lui kept falling over. There was too much stuffing in her pants.

"This simply increases my admiration for you, and my determination to make you my friend and colleague," Luc insisted. He seemed flustered—not quite as smooth as before. "We must have you at the High Table!"

The moment Luc said this, there it was: the High Table. The Great and the Good sat at its shiny mahogany surface, candlelight bouncing off silver and crystal, wood paneling behind them crawling partway to the sky. They were all there: the Military Men, a President, a Prime Minister, one or two Emperors, a Rock Star, and a Pope. They discussed the future of the Universe in the same serious sounding murmurs Lily had heard, as Snotty, in the Fortress of the Gnomes. There was one empty seat among them. In front of that empty seat was a place card stuck in a silver holder shaped like a swan. And that place card said, in calligraphic twirls: SNOTTY.

Lily was unimpressed. "Tried that one already, didn't you, Luc?" she said.

"Oh," Luc said hastily. "Sorry." When Lily looked again, the place card read "LILY" instead.

"How about it?" Luc said. Lily could hear him try not to whine.

"No, thanks," she said flatly. She turned her back on him again.

"Nonsense," Luc said in an over-hearty tone. "You've seen what you can do. You can command armies! And you're going to waste your talents on THESE?" At which he kicked Tuxton back over onto his snout in the sand.

Lily righted Tuxton. "You just don't get it, Luc, do you?" she said.

"What's that?" Luc said. She didn't answer. Snapping his fingers, he summoned up the Gnome Army. It appeared now as quickly as it had disappeared before. The Gnomes waited silently, waving their halberds and their scythes.

Lily looked them up and down. She looked Luc up and down. Luc's beautiful mouth twitched slightly as she did.

"So long, Luc," Lily said, and she turned away again, tucking the stuffed Tuxton up under one arm.

"Don't be ridiculous," Luc snapped. "Where can you possibly go?"

Lily shrugged. Carrying Tuxton, she walked away.

"I won't allow it," Luc said.

At this, Lily stopped. "YOU won't allow it?" she said, and she gave a short laugh. "That's a good one." She spun around and gave Luc one last look in the eye. "You were looking for me, weren't you?" she said softly. Her expression was bright with understanding. "All of them, all of this fighting, was just to keep me away from THEM." Her arm swept over the silent ranks of stuffed toys.

Luc made no answer.

"That's what I thought," Lily said.

But Luc wasn't finished yet. As history shows, in fact, he is never finished. He turned himself into a hundred foot tall fire-breathing Monster again, and blew a roaring stream of fire across Lily's path. "If you will not be for me," he thundered, and his voice shook the sky, "then you must be against me! SNOTTY! YOU! MUST! FIGHT!"

The Gnome Army goose-stepped in perfect formation, marching ever closer. The ground shook.

I'm not sure their hearts were in it, not really. Not even Luc's. Luc and his Gnome Army were just like anyone else, after all, in needing some kind of response, some kind of acknowledgement in order to keep going on in the same old way. And Lily's bored expression stopped them in their tracks.

Because Lily was right. In the end, the Weak are stronger than the Strong. Strange as it might seem, that is the way it has always been, and always will be, too.

Luc didn't know what to do. Making himself bigger didn't work. Neither did making himself louder, or grander, or even more terrifying. Yet these were the tricks that had won him all his battles for centuries past. Was he to change his tactics this late in the game? It didn't bear thinking of.

"Aren't you through YET?" Lily said coldly, as Luc breathed out clouds of red and violet steam through eight pairs of waving ivory tusks.

It was the last straw. With an aggrieved whine, Luc exploded into a shower of light, shattering into a thousand pieces, and scattering himself down to the desert floor.

As each piece of light touched one of the stuffed Toys, that Toy came back to life.

Snowflake and the Dog returned to their old selves.

Tia, Fia, Fion, Mion, Melia and Lui did cartwheels from joy at being able to move.

Tuxton wriggled down from Lily's arms. He pointed to the still advancing Grand Army of Gnomes. "Look!" he said in his high-pitched voice.

The Gnomes slowly froze where they stood. As Lily and the others watched, they turned into a ridge of granite, lining every horizon but the one taken up by the Mountains of Resistance. There the Gnomes turned to ash. A breeze blew the pale white stuff away.[74]

"HOORAY!" the Teddy Bear Army cheered. "Snotty saved the day! Snotty saved the day!"

"But...but I'm not Snotty!" Lily protested as Tia, Fia, Fion, Mion, Melia and Lui hoisted her on their shoulders. "I'm Lily!"

Still they all cheered her: "HOORAY FOR SNOTTY! HOORAY FOR SNOTTY! SNOTTY SAVED THE DAY!"

"Tuxton!" Lily yelled from where she bounced on the plush shoulders of her friends. "Tell them! It wasn't Snotty! It was me, Lily!" When this appeared to have no effect, she yelled as loudly as she could, "I'M LILY!"

At this, everyone was still. So quiet were they, in fact, that Lily could hear the wind as it bore away what was left of the ashes of the Gnomes.

Tuxton looked up at Lily with an earnest expression on his silly face. "But Lily," he said. "We KNOW that."

There was a pause.

"Well," Lily said finally, correcting herself. "I was Snotty, too, after all." And then, grudgingly, "He was okay, I guess."

At this a huge cheer went up. "HOORAY!" shouted the Teddy Bear Army as it surged forward. Lily fell backwards onto countless plush arms. "HOORAY! HOORAY! HOORAY!" And carrying Lily onto the Path of Care, all the Teddy Bears, and Snowflake, and the Dog stomped their feet and sang.

Everyone was as happy as it was possible for them to be. Because—

---

74   Is this how the mountains of Arcadia—the Donatees, the Samanthans, the Calandals, and, most beautiful of all, the Ceres—were formed?

of course—now was the time for a Teddy Bear Feast.[75]

---

75   Interesting note: The Teddy Bear Picnic is a common motif in folk tales of all worlds available for study, without exception. (See Vale, year 22; Vale, year 26.) There is scope for further study here that should fill younger scholars with excitement: how much are the stories of Arcadia like the stories of other worlds? And how much do the stories of those other worlds correspond to their own acknowledged realities? Are there other worlds as blind as ours to their true natures? Recent developments, encouraged by techniques nurtured by Sophia the Wise, have enabled us to peer through time and space to certain of these realities. We must communicate our own findings to them and seek to discover what laws they have themselves found. That is the next frontier for Arcadian science.

Chapter XXIII

A STARRY NIGHT

It was an excellent feast.

A picnic, of course, on the Meadow, in the Mountains, next to the Stream. A picnic is the best kind of feast when it's a warm summer's night.

At sunset, everyone was tired out, what with eating the many good things grilled on the giant celebration bonfire: the eggplant, the zucchini, the tomatoes, the onions, and the corn. There was hot apple cider and creamy hot chocolate for afterwards, and Tia, Fia, Fion, Mion, Melia and Lui entertained everyone with balalaika music, which they played very well and which was especially pleasant to listen to under the evening sky.

Mercy and Justice were there with another woman, older than them but even more beautiful. The two younger women treated her with the greatest respect. This was Truth, the Daughter of Time, and she was enjoying herself with her old friends. Lily was fascinated by the three women and wanted to speak to them. But she was shy and decided to wait for morning. "So much already happened today, what with withstanding the Forces of Evil and all." And she was happy sitting with Snowflake and the Dog and Tuxton—so happy that she never wanted the evening to end.

Then night fell, as night always does. Before the moon came up, the sky filled with a million stars.

One by one, the Teddy Bears yawned, stretched, and lay themselves out on pallets on the cool, springy grass of the meadow. One by one they fell asleep. Even Mercy and Justice, sitting with Truth, drowsed as Tia, Fia, Fion, Mion, Melia and Lui finished their last song and lay down for the night. Truth herself, who never sleeps, closed her eyes, and rested in her own deep thought.

All of the Toys and Animals and People yawned, falling asleep, one by one, under the brilliantly starry sky.

Just one bonfire was left, a small one, and that was the one around which sat the Dog, and Tuxton, and Snowflake, who nuzzled his head under Lily's arm. They drank steaming mugs of hot chocolate and whipped cream. The Dog lapped up his drink from a wide-mouthed bowl.

Tuxton toasted Lily. She ducked her head, embarrassed. But grinning shyly, she toasted him in return.

Lily yawned. She wanted to stay awake. She wanted to discuss the amazing events of the day, and to make plans. What would they do now, all of them? What brave and noble goals could they hope to achieve? What would they... what would they... what would they... what would they...

Lily tried to stay awake. But she had tired herself out enough, and, sliding into a well-earned rest, she put down her empty chocolate mug on the rush mats beside her, curled up on a blanket at Snowflake's side, and fell asleep.

Days have to come to an end. That's the way it is with them. And even heroes have to sleep sometime.

———————————

In the sky, with the rising of the moon, came one Star that even the moon's light couldn't withstand. This Star was more brilliant than all the others, and it blotted out the rest with its light.

Tuxton and the Dog and Snowflake, now the only ones awake in the whole of the sleeping camp, sat together in companionable silence. Every so often, Tuxton would stoke the fire. These were the

This Star was more brilliant than all the others,
and it blotted out the rest with its light.

only ones who saw the star. Tuxton pointed at it, quiet. The Dog, troubled, gave a quick nod. Snowflake said and did nothing, only gazed at it, steady, with his jewel-colored eyes.

They listened, for a moment, in the mountain silence.

Then they heard it. The distant flapping of wings.

As the Star came closer and closer, the sound, too, grew louder.

Snowflake's emerald eyes never left it, but the Dog exchanged a look with the silly-faced Bear. Both turned and looked at Lily, who lay sleeping by the fire. The Dog moved as if to guard her. The Star came closer and closer. Tuxton jumped up, too.

As the Star came into sight, the sound was explained. For she was an Angel. She was a beautiful, golden-brown skinned Angel, with sleek and shining black hair, deep black eyes, and delicate, pointed ears. She was well known to the three by the fire. They looked at her anxiously. As she landed on her light and graceful feet, Tuxton greeted her for them all.

"Star," Tuxton squeaked. "Hello, welcome." His voice sounded anxious, even to him, though he tried to keep it from seeming that way.

Star smiled at them all, warming her hands by the fire. Lily breathed evenly and smiled in her sleep. Still the three did not relax— Snowflake never took his eyes off the Angel, and Tuxton and the Dog exchanged uneasy looks. They shifted back and forth on their paws.

After a moment, the Angel straightened, as if she were going to do now what she had meant to all along. Her wings, which had folded when she landed, opened out now back to their full and glorious width. And she bent to gather Lily up in her arms.

"I was afraid of that," Snowflake said in a quiet voice, and a crystal teardrop fell from his eyes onto the meadow grass where it lay sparkling in the light from Star's eyes.

Tuxton just squeaked. "Does she...does she have to go, Star?" the Bear said in a timid voice. He put a paw out as if to touch his sleeping friend, then let it drop.

"Tuxton," Star said, and she smiled at the oddity of the name—she had known Tuxton by many different names in many different places and times, but of all of them, this was the silliest and the most endearing. "Tuxton, you know that all deeds done in one world affect all the others. You, of all creatures, know that well."[76]

"Yes," Tuxton said, still sad. "Of course I know that, Star."

"And would you have it any other way?"

Tuxton and the Dog looked at each other, and there was a flash of a second where they might have said that, yes, they would have liked it to be another way. Any other way that would keep and hold this moment. But the feeling passed by, and Tuxton shook his head.

"No, Star," he said. "I wouldn't have it any other way."

"She's due back in her own world," Star said, and her voice was sweet and sharp. "That's where she has to live."

"Will we... will we ever see each other again?" Tuxton asked. The Dog and Snowflake asked the same question with their eyes. "I mean, of course, in these forms. The way we've been together. It has been, for me, one of the best..." But here the Bear's voice trailed off, and he raised a plush paw to his eyes.

Star didn't wait for the end of the question. She knew she had no answer for it—even Angels can't know the Future, which no one knows but One—and she thought it best to take a little step, spring up, and then, before Tuxton had finished, to carry Lily well up into the night time sky.

As Star carried Lily away, the Dog and Snowflake looked after them, and Tuxton Ted waved one last farewell, until the Angel and the little girl were no more than specks in the dimly lit distance.

Star and Lily disappeared into the night sky.

---

76   The Law of the Interaction of Worlds is accepted as fact by most scholars. (See, even, Prof. Aspern Grayling, *Dominance and Hierarchy: First Principle Among Worlds*, New Power Press, year 52.)

"Mush!" he called as he disappeared into the night.

Chapter XXIV

DESPAIR, A BLOODY STUMP, AND A GLIMMER OF HOPE

Holding Lily in her arms, Star flew silently through the stars. There was the sound of jingling bells. A white-bearded man dressed in red velvet and white fur flew past, steering his reindeer-drawn sled into another part of the sky. Star nodded a greeting.

"Mush!" he called as he disappeared into the night. "Mush!"[77]

It began to snow.

The snow came down in slanting fat flakes, some in flurries swirled so forcefully by the wind that they looked like fat balls. There was so much snow that when Star turned toward Megalopolis she could only just see a faint flicker of the city lights.

Her wings flapped on. Star had flown through every kind of weather, on every kind of mission, to every kind of star, and to every kind of world. She was an Angel in her prime, the hope of the future, and when she had chosen to be guardian to Lily, her mentors had despaired.

"What!" they exclaimed. "A mean, nasty, ugly little brat like that?" There was anguish in heaven at the idea that she would throw herself away. For that was what it was to the older Angels: throwing herself

---

77   See Fallaize, year 61, for discussion of Santa's actual existence, and disappearance from activity in the physical world. Also see the Arcadian fairy tale, "Welcome to the Man in Red," told to Arcadian children at Christmas. Compare the Megalopolitan folk tale, a little known variation of "Anthony Saves the World," in which the hero outwits Santa in a battle for the affection of needy children. (See Vale, year 22.)

away.

There had been a time, of course, when every human in Megalopolis had an Angel to guide it. But that time was now long past. There were no Guardian Angels left on what was once called Earth—none, that is, until Lily was born. With her, the Angel made her plans. "That child's the Future," she said, serene. Of course this made her look foolish among her fellows. Over Lily, there was not much in the way of angelic competition.[78]

Star's thoughts were mysteriously her own, as she flew on and on, her wings beating steadily against the snow and the wind. She dipped down into the lower reaches of the atmosphere where the poisons of Megalopolis had accumulated and wrecked the sky. Through wisps of brown clouds she could see the vast city stretch out ahead. Star frowned.

But then, surprisingly, she smiled.

As she flew with the sleeping Lily in her arms, the brown clouds shriveled under an onslaught of snow falling from clouds even higher above. One by one, each was replaced by an eager white cloud. The harsh acquisitive lights that meant Megalopolis smoothed out and dimmed and mellowed, and then turned gold and warm.

Star smiled again and then, as if reminded of a nearly forgotten errand, she pulled up in her flight, her feet standing tiptoe on a cloud. She pivoted and turned. She flew past the lights of the great city until she was over the darkness of what was left of the planet's once vast ocean. She flew and flew until she could barely see the shore and then, judging she had flown far enough, she gave the sleeping Lily a gentle shake. Then another. Then another. And the Rose Gold Key tumbled out from Lily's pocket. Shining in the reflected light of Star's wings, it fell and fell and fell. Finally it reached the water below and with a quiet splash, disappeared.

---

78   Grayling insists this is allegory. Fallaize and Bender Boyce-Flood deny it, cautiously. I deny it utterly.

At this, Lily stirred and frowned in her sleep. But Star reached down and brushed the child's forehead with her lips. At this, two things happened: Lily settled into a deeper sleep than before. And Star had bound herself to Lily forever. Because that is the way it is with Angels.

Humming with pleasure now, Star made her way back to the shore. This time, she greeted the sight of Megalopolis without a wince, even as she dipped lower, searching for the filth of Hamercy Street. It might have been a trick of the winter light, but it seemed as if everywhere before her had changed.

And why shouldn't Star see Megalopolis as if it were a brand new place? Why shouldn't she see clusters of snug houses, separated by groves of trees and clear water, with people walking arm in arm through quiet streets, with good smells from brightly lit kitchens everywhere filling the air?[79]

Why not?

Even an Angel can dream.

And this was Christmas Eve.

––––––––––––

Spotting Hamercy Street, Star circled over the alley where Lily— or Snotty, as she had been—had hidden her treasure in the skip. A vast white blanket of unmarked snow covered that ugly thing, and everything else on the street as well.

Lightly she touched down next to the white mound that was the skip. Tenderly she laid Lily in the powdery snow.

And then she disappeared back up into the sky.

---

79   An accurate, even poetic, description of an Arcadian village street, at least before the Civil War. And of the childhood home of Lily the Silent, where she lived with her mother and stepfather, Mae and Alan, until the time of the adventure that transformed her into our first known queen.

"Huh? Hunh? WHAT?"

Lily, flailing at her face where the unfamiliar fat white flakes of snow fell, woke with a start.

To her surprise, she found she was almost covered with snow. Snow this deep and lasting was a rarity in Megalopolis. Lily shook it off. As she did, she called out, without thinking, "Tuxton? Snowflake? Melia!"

But there was no answer.

There was a pause. Lily's eyes, which looked more and more like Snotty's every minute that passed, snaked back and forth. She was still half asleep. She didn't know where she was. Or who she was, either.

"Tuxton! Snowflake!" she called out anxiously. "Where are you?" And then, doubtfully, "Melia? Are you there?"

Now Lily was awake. Her eyes widened. Slowly and horribly she realized where she was. She recognized the alley behind Hamercy Street. She recognized the skip, even under its cover of snow.

Lily's hand went to her mouth. She whimpered.

Suddenly she was up off the ground and running heavily through thick drifts of snow down the alley toward the Seventh Garden.

As she went she counted: One garden. Two gardens. Three. Four. Five...

Six.

There were only six gardens.

The Seventh Garden was gone. In its place was an empty, snow-covered lot.

Lily looked at this blankly. All of the events that led to Snotty's entering the Seventh Garden and falling down the Rabbit Hole, all of that came slowly back to her. Then she remembered Snotty's money.

"My money!" Lily gasped, looking more like Snotty than ever. Turning back, she ran to the skip. She burrowed frantically in the snow for Snotty's strongbox.

She found it there, lying on the ground, smashed. As she held it, its lid swung back creakily on its remaining hinge. It was empty.

"Oh no," Lily moaned. She shook the box, but it was no use. Snotty's money was gone.

Lily hurled the box face down in the snow and herself after it. She choked back a sob. "It must have been a dream," she told herself sternly. "The money, that's the important part." She hugged herself. "Only a dream," she repeated. But she still wanted to cry. Sniffling, she wiped her nose with the back of her hand. Then she stopped.

There was blood trickling down the side of her hand. Slowly she turned it so the palm faced up.

Where her little finger had been, only a bloody stump remained.

When she saw this, she said to herself, "I must have knocked it on the skip. Opened it up again."

But opened up what?

Lily sucked on the stump, trying to stop the blood. At this, all the memories of that other world down the Rabbit Hole came back. For a moment, warmed, she forgot the snow.

"Maybe," she muttered—and in that mutter was a gleam of hope—"maybe it wasn't a dream."

A glimmer of hope.

Lily furrowed her forehead and tried to make a plan.

Once again it began to snow.

Best was, she decided, to get on home. Then she could figure out how to find her way back through the Rabbit Hole.

Heartened by this thought, she began the trudge uphill through the high drifts of new fallen snow, back to the cold, mean little house where she had grown up.

That was when she remembered. It wasn't Lily who'd grown there. It was Snotty.

At this, she choked back another frightened sob.

How had she become Lily? She couldn't remember. But she knew that was who she was now. How was Lily to live in Snotty's place? There was no way. She knew that much. There was only one hope: she had to find her way back to the Seventh Garden.

But looking behind her, she knew the Seventh Garden was gone. And somehow—she didn't know how—Lily knew it was gone forever. It would never come back.

Lily thought that there was no way out. But she couldn't give up her hope just yet.

She couldn't give up hope because she didn't think she could bear it.

And there had to be a way. Otherwise, where was her little finger? Where had that gone?

There had to be hope. Lily believed that.

But as she struggled on through the snow, the glimmer of hope flickered, sputtered, and went out.

───────────

It was almost dawn when Lily turned up the steps of the house where she had grown up, and the porch light, shining through the lightly falling snow, was murky and dim. Lily remembered what life was like in that house, in Widdleshift, a neighborhood of Makewater, in the district of Hackendosh, part of the ancient county of Queerspittle, in the far northwest of East New York. She shuddered when she thought of it.

Letting herself in the front door, Lily crept up the stairs toward what had been her room—Snotty's room. She remembered how mean and cold it had been and, shivering, she pushed open its door. She fumbled for the greasy light switch she remembered well.

The light clicked on in Snotty's room.

Only—it wasn't Snotty's room now. It was Lily's. Where Snotty's room had mold clinging to its drab and peeling walls, Lily's room was bright and clean. The walls were a deep gold and the ceiling a pale sky blue covered with little golden stars. Instead of a cracked linoleum floor there was a warm rug, dark blue with a green sprig print, and on it there was a comfortable old chair. There was no broken electric fire lying in an empty grate. Instead a real fire burned cheerfully in a small white porcelain stove.

Next to the stove, in a snug corner of the room, there was a big brass bed, covered with a rose-colored quilt and a mound of pillows. And in the middle of the mound of pillows rested an enormous black and yellow teddy bear.[80]

"Big Teddy," she breathed. "Big Teddy!" And it really was the Noble Bear. Running to the bed, Lily grabbed Big Teddy up and hugged her, over and over, to her small chest.

"Big Teddy!" she exclaimed again. And, still clutching the Bear, she ran to the room's one dormer window.

She looked out. The sun had come out now, pushing through the clouds and lighting a pale blue sky. Lily looked at this and then looked down at the street below.

It was different, too. The dingy, horrible, mean little street where Snotty had grown up was gone.

Trees were everywhere now, growing along a nice wide pavement covered with snow. Lily saw neighbors greet each other as they came out of their homes. And there were benches on the street where they could sit. Lily saw her neighbors sitting on those benches, and others—these holding steaming mugs of something or other—coming out to join them. Lily saw the steam rise from the mugs. She opened the window and heard the neighbors exchange cheerful greetings. She felt the crisp, fresh air.

Shouts and laughter floated up toward Lily, and she looked down, astonished, over the schoolyard, to see her old friends playing there.

---

80   An exact replica of this room can be seen in the childhood home of Lily the Silent. The description is perfect, with the exception of the black and yellow bear.

Mick, Keef, and Dodger passed the time of day on a bench under a tall cedar tree, drinking mugs of cocoa and looking on.[81]

Lily shook her head in wonder. "Imagine that!" she murmured to Big Teddy. Then she stuck her head out farther into the clear, cold air, and looked down into the alley behind Hamercy Street.

The gardens there, now covered with snow, looked like the gardens in a winter fairy tale. But there was no Seventh Garden. Lily had hoped against hope that she would find it again. But she didn't. And she never did.

---

81 Arcadian census records of the year 1 show a Mick, a Keef, and a Dodger living in the neighborhood of Lily the Silent's childhood home. The three (the names are unusual for Arcadia) appear to have owned an eponymous neighborhood sweet shop.

Chapter XXV

CHRISTMAS DAY

It was Christmas Day on Hamercy Street, which is in the village of Cockaigne, which is part of the necklace of towns known as Arcadia. Arcadia, as is well known throughout the worlds, is a happy place, and Christmas Day is one of the happiest of its year.[82]

In the house at the top of Hamercy Street, Lily's mother Mae served Christmas breakfast to Lily and to Alan. He and Mae were going to be married, so it was a very jolly breakfast, even for Christmas Day.[83] There were dried cherry scones dripping with butter. There were fat sausages sizzling on the griddle. There were sweet oranges and crisp apples and walnuts in their shells. And for the pudding there was chocolate covered marzipan.

Afterwards, Alan did the washing up while he and Mae talked, and Lily knelt down to play with her Christmas gift from Alan. This was a shaggy gray and black puppy, and Lily, the moment she saw him, knew who he was.

"Dog?" she said, looking into his brown eyes. The puppy squirmed and licked her on the end of her nose.

It was the Dog. Lily was sure. She looked at him in wonder, setting him carefully down on the floor. He waddled there contentedly and then, sitting down, he yawned. She looked at him (as Alan and Mae

---

82   Of course this is true of Arcadia, or was in the time before the Civil War began.

83   As has already been remarked, Alan and Mae are common names in Arcadian history. They are also the names of the magistrate who was mother to Lily the Silent, and her second husband, Alan the Freedom Fighter, son of the famous Freedom Fighter Maud Delilah.

looked on, pleased at the success of the gift), and she looked at Big Teddy who sat propped up on the stairs. And she thought, "Yes. It was real. It wasn't a dream." There would be a way back. The Dog and Big Teddy would help her to find it. She was sure of that now.

The puppy barked.

"Rex," Lily said. "Your name is Rex." She was sure of this, too.

Lily didn't know it, but the Dog's name had been Rex.[84]

So she went out to play, with Rex at her heels, into the crisp air of Hamercy Street. Outside there was the smell of a hundred Christmas breakfasts, of hot cocoa and cream, of evergreen wreaths and oranges and cloves. The breeze brushed her face. She turned toward the new, bright schoolyard, from where she could hear the laughing voices of her friends as they played.

But Lily didn't go there, not just yet. First she went to the row of houses in front of the gardens of Back Hamercy Street. They were neat and comfortable now, and in front of each one was a little smiling plaster Gnome.

———————

"BBBBBBZZZZZZTTTTTTT."

It was still there. She had known it would be. But she wanted to see it for herself. The phone mast.

"BBBBZZZZZTTTTTT."

Lily looked at the tower. It stood there, mean looking and shabby, its base wrapped with barbed wire and glass coated string.

"BBBBZZZZTTTTTT."

Rex whined and pushed up against Lily's ankle. He gave a guttural little growl.

The stump of Lily's little finger began to throb.

---

84 Lily the Silent often spoke of her dog, Rex, killed in the great Megalopolitan occupation of year 3 (private conversation with the editor).

"BBBBZZZZTTTTT," went the phone mast, and there was a shower from it of blue sparks. They fell in a graceful arc from the top down to the snowy pavement beneath. And when they landed, standing there where they had been was the most beautiful young man in the world. He looked up. His turquoise blue eyes looked deep into Lily's own.

"You're still here," she whispered. And he nodded, amused. In the next moment he was gone.

A chill wind swept down the street. Lily shivered and, picking up a quivering Rex, hugged him to her coat. Still holding the puppy, she slowly turned toward the playground.

Her friends ran to meet her and, exclaiming over Rex, showed off their own gifts, too. Lily, chattering, back where she belonged, told herself she could worry about that other little matter tomorrow.

Today was Christmas. She would worry about the Enemy another day.

So Lily and a barking Rex joined in the game. And Star, flying back to the heavens overhead, saw this and was glad. The Angel flew over the changed city and saw, not the sterile magnificence of Megalopolis, but Arcadia, its villages divided prettily by fields and trees. But she saw farther than that—farther than Lily, from her window at the top of Hamercy Street, could.

She saw that Megalopolis had been beaten back, but not beaten, and that the ground won by the green and healthy strand of towns was this much and no more. Megalopolis still surrounded Arcadia, grim and menacing, and angry at the challenge that the villages presented to its cold grandeur.[85]

---

85 A final note: That stories are real has been proven by Arcadian art and science, though not without violent dissent. That people can only see what they already believe has also been proven as physical fact. The only possible breach to this wall of familiar prejudice is a new idea, though it is accepted that this is extremely rare. For example, the story of Snotty could be an actual history of the birth of Arcadia.

Star, as she flew on, was troubled by the idea that there would come a time—and that very soon—when the Battle would have to be fought all over again. There would, at that time, be this change: that she and her allies would start with an inch or two more ground, just a little more advantage, than when she had last set out. No more. With this, the Angel was forced to be content.

What Lily felt, Star knew: that the fight would come again.

For now, though, it was Christmas Day in Arcadia. And Star allowed herself, for the moment, to be pleased.

THE END

This would solve the age-old problem in Arcadian physics of our country's lack of history from before year 1. And yet, the evidence could be there for all to see, but all would be unable to see, as such a story is out of our experience. It would need another eye—even the eye of another culture, one observing the story with greater objectivity—to introduce the new idea before the story could be seen for what it, in fact, actually is. And this would agree with the new discoveries about the importance of Interactive Partnership in the development of healthy culture (see work being done by students at Hanuman School of Healing, in collaboration with Yuan Mei College).

I mention this now, not as a theoretical possibility, but as a fact. I believe, and say here, that Arcadia was formed by Snotty discovering and accepting who he really is. I believe that Snotty was our first queen, Lily the Silent. I am fully aware of the potential political explosiveness of this idea at this time. But times change. And Truth, of course, is the Daughter of Time. (For discussion of actual personifications of Truth and Time, see Bender Boyce-Flood, year 62.) I rest my conclusions, and my lifetime of scholarship on . . .

A Note from Dr. Alan Fallaize

Professor Vale's notes stop there, incomplete. The afterword she had planned as a formal analysis of the material was never written.

I have attached a short bibliography of works mentioned in the text, for use by the casual reader. Scholars will find complete records at the Archives, Eisler Hall, Amaurote. Contact Professor Daisy Fallaize, Chief Archivist.

In this year of Sophia the Wise, 83 AE
The Tower By The Pond

An Incomplete List of Publications by Arcadian Scholars
(published by Otterbridge University Press, unless otherwise noted)

year 14, *An Elegant Theory of the Contiguity of Theater Arts and Neurobiology*, Prof. Chloe Watson.

year 17, *History or Physics: A False Dichotomy*, Prof. Joyanna Bender Boyce-Flood.

year 22, *Folk Tales of Megalopolis and Arcadia: A Comparative Study*, Prof. Devindra Vale.

year 25, *Journey to the Center of an Illusion*, Prof. Joyanna Bender Boyce-Flood.

year 26, *A Short History of the Fairy Tale (with excerpts from the Legendus Snottianicus)*, Prof. Devindra Vale.

year 34, *Legendus Snottianicus: translations of fragments of an Arcadian folk tale*. Translated by Prof. Joyanna Bender Boyce-Flood, with notes by Prof. Devindra Vale.

year 41, *Twelve Points Against the Existence of Unity*, Prof. Aspern Grayling.

year 43, *The Siegfried Cycle*, edited by Prof. Aspern Grayling. New Power Press.

year 52, *Dominance and Hierarchy: First Principle Among Worlds*, Prof. Aspern Grayling. New Power Press.

year 54, *The Legendus Snottianicus: The More We Know the Less We Understand*, Prof. Devindra Vale.

year 59, *Connection: A Personal Journey of Discovery, Loss, and Love*, Dr. Malcolm Sivia.

year 61, *On the Discovery of Biological Truths in Fairy Tales*, Dr. Alan Fallaize, with foreword by Prof. Devindra Vale.

year 62, *Storyland: Storehouse in the Ether?*, Prof. Joyanna Bender Boyce-Flood.

year 76, *Catalog of the* Analecta Arcadia *and the* Acta Arcadia, compiled by Prof. Joyanna Bender Boyce-Flood.

year 83, *The Annotated* Snotty Saves The Day, foreword and notes by Prof. Devindra Vale, edited by Dr. Alan Fallaize.

Praise for Dr. Alan Fallaize's
ON THE DISCOVERY OF BIOLOGICAL TRUTHS IN FAIRY TALES...

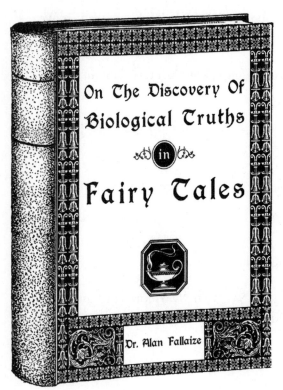

"Dr. Fallaize tells us in simple, clear language what most of us knew in our hearts: our stories tell us who we are..."
—*The Arcadian Journal of Teaching, Cooking, & Engineering*

"...a modern classic...almost a detective story of a great scientific discovery..." —*The Wrykyn Review*

"Brilliantly conceived, eminently readable, an achievement by a great scholar. Three cheers for Fallaize!" —*Physics Today*

Excerpts from Dr. Alan Fallaize's classic work,
ON THE DISCOVERY OF BIOLOGICAL TRUTH IN FAIRY TALES...

A man in a church sees a pink and gold animal resembling a boar, with violets and roses growing out of its tusks. Does he really see this? Does it really exist?

A mathematician sees a white rabbit run across a field holding a pocket watch. Is the rabbit really there? And what time is it anyway?

A woman praying in a chapel in the far off world of Spain levitates above the ground, annoying her fellow worshippers with an excess of piety. Did she really rise up? Is it a mass hallucination? And why do they all dislike her so much?

These are the kinds of questions that we, the adherents of the New Science, began to ask ourselves. In many ways, they are a sign of both how lost we were, and how determined we were not to follow the error filled paths of the past.

And the answers, doggedly arrived at, surprised us.

Available at finer booksellers from
OTTERBRIDGE UNIVERSITY PRESS

TOD DAVIES, founder of *EXTERMINATING ANGEL PRESS*,
firmly believes in the truth of fairy tales,
and that if you know who you are,
(and what made you that way),
you can change your world, too.